Rachel Wells is a mother, writer and cat lover. She lives in Devon with her family and her pets and believes in the magic of animals. Rachel grew up in Devon but lived in London in her twenties working in marketing and living in a tiny flat with an elderly rescued cat, Albert. After having a child she moved back to Devon and decided to take the plunge and juggle motherhood with writing.

She has always wanted to write and now has found her voice in her first novel, *Alfie the Doorstep Cat*. She has always had cats as pets, ever since a young child, and she has always wanted to write. Rachel is delighted to have been able to combine her two main passions at last.

# ALFIE
## The Doorstep Cat

### Rachel Wells

**AVON**

AVON

A division of HarperCollins*Publishers*
1 London Bridge Street,
London SE1 9GF

www.harpercollins.co.uk

This paperback edition 2015

A catalogue record for this book is
available from the British Library

ISBN 978-0-00-813315-3

Set in Bembo Std by Ben Gardiner

Printed and bound by CPI Group (UK) Ltd, Croydon, CR0 4YY

MIX
Paper from
responsible sources
FSC
www.fsc.org   FSC C007454

This book has been a pleasure to write because of the team I have been privileged enough to work with. Thanks especially go to my wonderful Editor, Helen Bolton; this process has been so much fun and you have been inspiring, encouraging and a wonderful guide in my first novel. Also the team at Avon have all been so excited for this which has driven me on immensely. I have also been lucky to have fantastic agents, so big thanks go to Kate Burke and all at Diane Banks Associates.

My family have been a great source of encouragement, keeping me fed and letting me write late into the night. My wonderful friends have kept me grounded as I ran ideas past them – I feel you have all been a part of this.

Finally to the cats who have been part of my family throughout my life. This is for all of you; you've been my family, my friends, my inspiration and at many times my support. You aren't just pets, you are so much more.

*To Ginger, my first cat who I took on walks on his lead and let me treat him as if he was a doll. You are long gone but never forgotten.*

# Chapter
# One

Chapter
One

'It's not going to take too long to pack up the house,' Linda said.

'Linda, you're so optimistic; look at all the junk your mother collected,' Jeremy replied.

'That's unfair. She's got some nice china and you never know, some of it might be worth something.'

I was pretending to be asleep but my ears were pricked up, listening to what was being said as I tried to stop my tail flicking in agitation. I was curled up on Margaret's favourite chair – or rather, the chair that had been her favourite – watching her daughter and son-in-law discuss what would happen; determining my future. The past few days had been so terrifyingly confusing, especially as I didn't fully understand what had happened. However, what I did understand as I listened, trying my best not to cry, was that life would never be the same again.

'You'll be lucky. Anyway, we should call a house clearance place. Lord knows we don't want any of her stuff.' I tried to sneak a look without them noticing. Jeremy was tall, grey haired and bad tempered. I had never really liked him, but the woman, Linda, had always been nice to me.

'I'd like a chance to keep a few of Mum's things. I'll miss her.' Linda started crying and I yearned to yowl along with her, but I kept quiet.

'I know, love,' Jeremy's voice softened. 'It's just that we can't stay here forever. Now the funeral's over, we need to think about getting the house on the market and, well, if we get it packed up, we can be off in a few days.'

'It just seems so final, though. But you're right, of course.' She sighed. 'And what about Alfie?' I bristled. This was what I was waiting for. What would happen to me?

'We need to put him in a shelter I suppose.' I felt my fur stand on end.

'A shelter? But Mum loved him so much. It seems so cruel to just get rid of him.' I wished I could voice my agreement with her; it was beyond cruel.

'But you know we can't take him home. We've got two dogs, love. A cat just won't work for us, you know that.'

I was incensed. It wasn't that I wanted to go with them, but I absolutely couldn't go to a shelter.

*Shelter.* My body shuddered at the word; such an inappropriate name for what we in the cat community thought of as 'death row'. There might be a few lucky cats who got re-homed, but then who knew what happened to them? Who was to say that the family that re-homed them would treat them well? The cats I knew unanimously agreed that a shelter was a bad place. And we knew full well that for those that weren't re-homed, the death sentence loomed.

Although I considered myself a handsome cat with a certain kind of charm, there was no way I was going to take that risk.

'I know you're right, the dogs would eat him alive. And they're very good at these shelters these days, so he might be re-homed quickly.' She paused as if she was still mulling things over. 'No, it has to be done. I'll call the shelter in the morning and the house clearance company. Then I guess we can get an estate agent round.' She sounded more sure of herself and I knew my fate had been sealed unless I did something about it.

'Now you're thinking straight. I know this is hard, but Linda, your mum was very old and honestly, it's not like it was a huge surprise.'

'That doesn't make it easy though, does it?'

I put my paws over my ears. My little head was reeling. In the past two weeks I had lost my owner, the only human I'd ever really known. Life had been turned upside down and I was heartbroken, desolate and now, it seemed, homeless. What on earth was a cat like me supposed to do?

I was what was known as a 'lap cat'. I didn't feel the need to be out all night hunting, prowling or socialising, when I had a warm lap, food and comfort. I also had company; a family. But then it was all taken away, leaving my cat heart totally broken. For the first time ever I was all alone.

I had lived in this small terraced house with my owner, Margaret, almost my whole life. I also had a sister cat called Agnes, although she was more like an aunt, being so much older than me. When Agnes went to cat heaven, a year ago, I felt a pain that I had never thought possible. It hurt so much that I didn't think I would ever recover. But I had Margaret, who loved me very much, and we clung together in our grief. We had both adored Agnes and we missed her with every ounce of our beings, united in our suffering.

However, I recently learnt how incredibly cruel life could be. One day, a couple of weeks ago, Margaret didn't get up from her bed. I had no idea what was wrong or what to do, being a cat, so I lay next to her and yowled as loudly as I could. Luckily, a nurse who came to see Margaret once a week was due, and when I heard the doorbell I reluctantly left Margaret's side and leapt out of the cat flap.

'Oh my, what's wrong?' the nurse asked, as I wailed for all I was worth. When she pushed the doorbell again, I pawed at her, gently but insistently trying to convey that something was wrong. She used the spare key and found Margaret's life-less body. I stayed with Margaret, knowing she was lost to me, as the nurse made some phone calls. After a while, some men came to take her away and I couldn't stop yowling. They wouldn't let me go with Margaret, and that was when I real-ised that my life, as I knew it, was over. Margaret's family were called and I yowled some more. I yowled myself hoarse.

As Jeremy and Linda continued talking, I quietly jumped off the chair and left the house. I prowled around looking for some of the other cats to ask advice from, but it was pretty much tea time so I struggled to find anyone. However, I knew a nice elderly cat called Mavis who lived down the street, so I went to seek her out. I sat outside her cat flap and miaowed loudly. She knew that Margaret had died; she'd seen her being taken away and had found me shortly afterwards pining after her. She was a maternal cat, a bit like Agnes, and she had taken care of me, letting me yowl until I could yowl no more. She had stayed with me, sharing her food and milk with me, until Linda and Jeremy arrived.

Hearing my call, she came out of the cat flap, and I explained the situation to her.

'They can't take you?' she asked, looking at me with sad eyes.

'No, they say they have dogs and, well, I don't want to live with dogs anyway.' We both shivered at the thought.

'Who would?' she said.

'I don't know what to do,' I lamented, trying not to cry again. Mavis nestled her body into me. We hadn't been close until recently, but she was a very caring cat, and I was grateful for her friendship.

'Alfie, don't let them take you to the shelter,' she said. 'I'd take care of you but I don't think I can. I'm old and tired now and my owner isn't much younger than Margaret was. You have to be a brave little cat and find yourself a new family.' She rubbed her neck into mine affectionately.

'But how do I do that?' I asked. I had never felt so lost or scared.

'I wish I had the answers, but think what you have learnt lately about how fragile life is, and be strong.'

We rubbed noses, and I knew that I had to leave. I went back to Margaret's house one last time so I could remember it before I left. I wanted a picture to lock in my memory and take on my journey with me. I hoped it might give me strength. I looked at Margaret's trinkets, her 'treasures' she called them. I looked at the pictures on the wall that had been so familiar to me. I looked at the carpet, worn where I had scratched at it when I was too young to know better. This house was me, and I was it. And now I had no idea what was to become of me.

I had little appetite but I forced myself to eat the food that Linda had given me (after all I wasn't sure when I would get to eat next), and then I took one final, lingering look around the home that had been mine; that had always kept me warm and safe. I thought about the lessons I'd learnt. In my four years in this house I had grasped a lot about love, and about loss. I had once been taken care of, but not any longer. I remembered the time I arrived as a tiny kitten. How Agnes hadn't liked me and had treated me as a threat. How I had won her round, and how Margaret had always treated us as if we were the most important cats in the world. I thought about how lucky I had been; but now my luck had run out. As I mourned the only life that I had known, I felt instinctively that I had to survive, but I had no idea how. I prepared to take a leap into the unknown.

# Chapter Two

With my broken heart, and fearing no reasonable alternative, I set out from the only home I'd ever known. I had no idea where I was going, or how I was going to manage, but I knew that relying on myself, and my limited abilities, would be better than relying on a shelter. And I also knew that a cat like me needed to have a home and love. As I crept off into the dark night, my little body shaking with fear, I tried to find a way to be brave. I knew little but I was certain that I didn't ever want to be alone again. This cat desperately needed to find a lap, or even a number of laps, to sit on. With a sense of purpose, I tried to muster my courage. I hoped, prayed, that it wouldn't fail me.

I started walking, letting my senses guide me. I wasn't used to prowling the streets in the dark, unwelcoming night, but I could see and I could hear well and kept telling myself that it would be all right. I tried to hear Margaret and Agnes' voices as I walked the streets, to drive me on.

The first night was hard – frightening and long. At some point, as the moon shone down, I found a shed at the bottom of someone's back garden, which was lucky because my legs were hurting and I was exhausted. The door was open, and although it was dusty and full of cobwebs, I was too tired to care. I curled up in a corner on the hard, dirty floor, but somehow I managed to fall fast asleep.

I was awoken during the night by a loud yowl, and a large black cat loomed over me. I jumped into the air in fright. He stared at me angrily, and although my legs were shaking, I tried to stand my ground.

'What are you doing here?' he hissed, spitting at me aggressively.

'I just needed to sleep,' I replied, trying and failing to sound confident. There was no way I could get past him easily, so, trembling, I stood up and tried to look menacing. The cat grinned, an evil grin, and I nearly buckled. He reached out and swiped my head with his claws. I yelped and felt the pain from where he'd scratched me and I wanted to curl into a ball but knew that I had to get away from this vicious cat. He came at me again, claws glinting, brandished at my face, but luckily I was more agile than him. I launched myself towards the door and ran past him, brushing his wiry fur but managing to get outside. He turned and hissed at me again. I spat back then ran as fast as my little legs would take me. At some point, I stopped and breathlessly looked back to find I was alone. I had had my first taste of danger and I knew that I needed to develop a thicker fur if I was going to make it. I used my paw to smooth my coat and tried to ignore the scratch, which still smarted. I realised that I could be fast when I needed to be, and that was something I could use to get myself out of danger. I yelped some more as I walked on, fear flooding through me, but also driving me. I looked into the night sky, at the stars, and wondered, yet again, if Agnes and Margaret could see me, wherever they were. I hoped so, but I didn't know. I knew very little.

I was so hungry by the time I felt able to stop again and it was very cold. Used to sitting by Margaret's fire day after day, this was an alien life to me. I knew that if I needed food I would have to hunt; something I hadn't had to do very much of in my past and something I wasn't adept at. I followed my nose and found some mice skulking around the bins outside a big house. Despite my distaste – I usually ate food from a tin, except on special occasions when Margaret gave me fish – I chased one into a corner and went in for the kill. Because I hadn't been used to hunger like this, it tasted almost delicious to me and it gave me the energy that I needed to continue.

I wandered on through the night until the day began to dawn, trying to remember that I was still me, Alfie, the playful cat, as I chased my tail and practised my bounding. I hunted a fat fly, but then I remembered I needed to conserve my energy; I didn't know where my next meal would come from or when I'd get it.

Still with no idea where I was heading, I came to a big road and realised I would need to cross it. I wasn't used to roads and traffic; Margaret had lectured me about not going near roads when I was a kitten. It was noisy and scary as cars and vans zoomed past me. I stood on the pavement, my heart pounding, until I saw a gap. I almost closed my eyes and ran, but managed to steady my shaking legs before I did anything stupid. Fearfully, I put one little paw down onto the road, feeling the rumble of traffic as it grew nearer. A horn blared and as I turned to my left I saw an enormous pair of lights bearing down on me. I bolted, running faster than I ever had in my life, and to my horror I felt something brush my tail. I yelped and leapt as far as I could, landing on the pavement. Heart beating, I turned around and saw a car speed past, knowing I had nearly ended up under it. I wondered if I had used up one of my nine lives – I was pretty sure I had. Eventually I caught my breath, again fear was becoming my driving force, and legs like jelly, I walked for a few minutes away from the road, before I collapsed by someone's front gate.

After a few minutes, a door opened and a lady came out.

She had a dog with her, on a lead. The dog lurched at me, barking wildly, and once again I had to dodge out of harm's way. The lady yanked the lead and shouted at the dog, who snarled at me. I hissed back.

I was learning very quickly that the world was a dangerous and hostile place, a million miles away from my home, Agnes and Margaret. I began to wonder if a shelter wouldn't have been safer after all.

However, there was no going back. By now I had no idea where I was. When I first set out, I didn't know exactly where I was going or what would happen to me but I had my hopes. I thought I would have to travel a bit but in the back of my mind, a kind family, perhaps a sweet little girl, would find me and take me to my new home. As I faced daily terrors, sometimes running for my life, and often feeling like I was ready to collapse from hunger, this was the picture I kept in my head.

By now, I was disorientated, thirsty and tired. The adrenaline that had kept me going was deserting me and being replaced by a heaviness in my limbs.

I found my way to a back alley, where, if I jumped on fences and balanced like a ballerina, I could make my way along, looking down from high enough to feel safe. I tapped into my energy reserves in order to do so. I spotted a garden with a big bowl of water on a post; Margaret had had one in her garden for birds to drink from. I jumped down and managed to climb up it, so desperate for a drink that I would have climbed the highest mountain. I drank greedily, grateful for the immediate relief it gave me. I swiped some birds away; this was my water now. When I had all but emptied it, I returned to the fences and made my way further and further away from my old life.

I spent a thankfully uneventful night. I met some other cats but they ignored me, too concerned with their cat calling and mating to pay much heed.

Most of what I knew about other cats, I had learnt from Agnes, who could hardly move by the time I met her, and the other cats on our street, who were generally friendly, especially Mavis, who had shown me such kindness. I wanted to approach the cats to ask for help, but they looked too busy and I was scared after the black cat incident, so I trotted on carefully.

The next morning, I felt as if I had come quite a distance. Yet again I was hungry, so I decided that I would try to look my most appealing in the hope that some kindly cat would help me out with food. I happened upon a cat who was basking in the sunshine outside a house with a shiny red door. I tentatively approached and purred.

'Goodness,' said the cat, who was a rather large lady tabby. 'You look dreadful.' I was about to take offence but I remembered that I hadn't really groomed myself properly since leaving Margaret's due to the fact I was more concerned with staying alive and out of trouble.

'I'm homeless and hungry,' I miaowed.

'Come on, I'll share some of my breakfast with you,' she offered. 'But then you'll have to go. My owner will be home soon and won't like to find a stray in her house.' It suddenly struck me that I really was a stray. I had no home, no family, no protection. I was among the unfortunate cats that had to fend for themselves; living in fear, always feeling hungry and tired. Never feeling quite their best; never looking anything near their best. I had now joined their ranks and it felt horrible.

I gratefully ate and drank and then went on my way, thanking and bidding farewell to the kindly cat. I didn't even know her name.

My state of mind reflected my physical being. Grief was such a part of me; causing me physical pain in my heart as I missed Margaret with every fibre of my fur. But I had known love; the love of my owner and my cat sister, and I owed it to them, to their love, to carry on. Now, with food in my tummy, I felt renewed energy as I prepared to do just that.

# Chapter
# Three

A few days passed, increasing the distance between my old home and wherever I was heading. I met some kind cats, some angry ones, and many mean dogs that delighted in barking at me but thankfully couldn't get me. I was kept on my toes, literally, as I danced and jumped and ran away, and I could feel my energy depleting all the time. I learnt to fight back when I needed to; although aggression didn't come naturally to me, it seemed survival did. As I dodged cars, cats and dogs, I was slowly developing a more streetwise persona.

However I was getting thinner by the day; my once gleaming fur was patchy and I was cold and tired. I barely knew how I was surviving and I had never imagined that life could ever be like this. I was sadder than I had ever been and more lonely than I thought possible. When I slept, I had nightmares, and when I woke, I remembered my predicament and cried. It was a horrible time and sometimes I just wanted it all to be over. I wasn't sure how much longer I could carry on.

I was learning that the streets could be mean and unforgiving. Physically and mentally it was taking its toll on me and I was beginning to feel so downhearted that it was a struggle to put one paw in front of the other.

The weather reflected my mood. It was cold and raining, and I felt a chill in my bones as my fur never seemed to be fully dry. In the time that I had been homeless – searching for my future, the kind family – the sweet little girl hadn't materialised. No one had come to my rescue so far and I was beginning to think that no one would. To say I was feeling sorry for myself was an understatement.

Once again, I came to a main road. Roads still filled me with fear; I'd got better at crossing them, but I still felt as if I was taking my life in my paws every time I stepped off a kerb. I had learnt to take my time when crossing, even if I had to wait for a very long time. So I sat, head moving side to side until there was a break in the traffic that made it safe enough. Despite this I still ran as fast as I could and ended up breathless on the other side. Unfortunately, I had been so busy concentrating on getting across the road that I hadn't noticed the small fat dog standing on the other side of the road. He squared up to me, snarling, showing his sharp teeth and dribbling saliva. Unfortunately there was no lead or owner in sight.

'Hisssss,' I replied, trying to deter him, although I was terrified. He was so close to me I could smell him. He barked at me and suddenly lunged forward. Despite my fatigue I leapt back and started running, but I could feel his breath on my tail. Increasing my speed I dared to look back and could see him coming after me, snapping at my heels. For such a fat dog he was quick and I could hear him barking furiously as I ran. I rounded a corner and came upon an alleyway. I swerved and sprinted down it as fast as my legs would take me. After what felt like miles I slowed and hearing only silence I looked back; thankfully the dog was nowhere to be seen. I'd managed to escape.

Heart pounding, I slowed my pace, and made my way down the alley which led to some allotments where people grew vegetables. As it was still pouring with rain there were only a couple of people about, so despite my dampness and fatigue, I strode confidently to find shelter. One of the allotments had a shed with a door that was slightly ajar. I was too tired to worry about what might lie in wait inside, and gently nudged the door open with my nose. I was so cold and insecure, I feared that if I didn't find somewhere dry to rest soon I would become very sick.

I slunk into the shed and was grateful to see a blanket at one end. It was musty and a bit rough; it certainly wasn't the luxury I had been used to in my old life but at that moment in time it was like a palace to me. I curled up and tried to rub my fur dry as best I could, and despite being half-starved, I couldn't face going to find any food.

I could hear the rain hitting the shed as I cried, silently to myself. I had always been a very spoilt cat, I saw that now. If I thought of all the things I took for granted when I lived with Margaret, it was a very long list. I knew I would be fed, loved, warm and cared for. I spent cold days sitting by a warm fire in Margaret's living room. I spent cold days sunning myself by the window. I was mollycoddled and my life was one of pure luxury. It was funny how it was only now it was gone that I realised how lucky I had been.

And now what was to become of me? When Mavis had told me to leave I really didn't foresee what would happen. I didn't think I would be here, wondering if I could carry on. I really wasn't sure that I could continue. Was my journey going to end here in this shed, on a smelly blanket? Was that my fate? I hoped not, yet I didn't know what the alternative was. I knew that feeling sorry for yourself was wrong but I couldn't help it. I missed my old life so badly and I just didn't know what would become of me.

I must have fallen asleep because I was awoken by a pair of eyes staring at me; I blinked. There was a cat stood in front of me, as black as night, eyes shining like torches.

'I don't mean any harm,' I said immediately, thinking that if she wanted to fight I would let her finish me off.

'I thought I smelt a cat. What are you doing here?' she asked, although not aggressively.

'I wanted to rest. A dog chased me and I just ended up here. It was warm and dry and so ...'

'Are you a street cat?' she asked.

'I'm not supposed to be but I guess I am at the moment,' I replied sadly. She arched her back.

'Look, this is my hunting ground. I'm a street cat and I like it that way. I get the rich pickings of the creatures that come here looking for food - mice, birds you know, anyway, I kind of call this my patch. I just wanted to check that you didn't think you could take it over.'

'Of course not!' I was indignant. 'I just needed shelter from the rain.'

'You get used to the rain eventually,' she said. I wanted to say, 'perish the thought,' but I didn't want to upset my new comrade. I slowly stood up and moved toward her.

'Does it get easier?' I asked, wondering if this really was my future.

'I don't know, but you get accustomed to it.' Her eyes darkened. 'Anyway, come with me I'll let you hunt with me and I'll show you where to get a drink but then, in the morning you move on OK?' I agreed her terms.

I ate and drank but I didn't feel better. As I curled up on the blanket again, and my new friend left me, I prayed for a miracle because as things stood I didn't think I would come out of this journey alive.

# Chapter
# Four

Chapter
Four

I set off again the next morning as promised, but I felt despondent. As a few more days passed I experienced a mass of contradictions. One day I would feel I couldn't carry on; the weather, the hunger and the loneliness would get to the core of me. But then the next I would push myself further, telling myself I owed it to Margaret and Agnes not to give up. I would see-saw between feeling hopeless in my quest or determined not to fail.

I got by with food and drink, and learnt to be more self-sufficient. I even began to get used to the weather although I still hated the rain. I hunted slightly more effectively, although I didn't enjoy it, but I had discovered how to be a little bit tougher. I was just not convinced I really could be as resilient as I needed to be. Not yet.

One night, feeling in a more positive frame of mind, I came across a group of humans. They were all huddled around a large doorway; there was lots of cardboard and it smelt very bad. They all had bottles in their hands and some of them had almost as much fur on their faces as me.

'It's a cat,' one of the furry men slurred, taking a drink. He waved his bottle towards me; the stench sent me reeling back. They laughed as I started slowly moving backwards, not sure what danger I was facing, if any. The man who laughed then threw a bottle at me, I dodged it but only just as it smashed to pieces next to me.

'It'd make a nice hat to keep me warm,' another laughed, slightly menacingly, I thought. I crept further back.

'We ain't got no food, bugger off,' a third said, unkindly.

'We could skin 'im for a hat then eat 'im,' another said, laughing. I widened my eyes in horror and backed away. Then, from nowhere, a cat appeared.

'Follow me,' he hissed, and I ran after him down the street. Thankfully, just as I thought I couldn't run any more, we stopped.

'Who were they?' I asked, breathlessly.

'Neighbourhood drunks. They don't have homes. You should keep away from them.'

'But I don't have a home either,' I cried, and I felt like yowling again.

'I'm sorry to hear that. But you should still keep out of their way. They aren't exactly friendly.'

'What's drunk?' I asked, feeling very much like a little cat with no idea about the world yet again.

'It's something humans do. They drink stuff and it changes them. Not milk or water. Look, come with me. I can sneak you some food and milk tonight and find you somewhere safe to sleep.'

'You're very kind,' I purred.

'I've been where you are; I was homeless for a while,' the cat said, and then stalked off, gesturing with his paw for me to follow him.

His name was Button, which he said was a silly name for a cat but he had a young owner who said he was 'cute as a button', whatever that means. The house we went to was in darkness and I was so happy to be inside, somewhere warm and safe. It reminded me that I desperately needed to find a home before long. I told Button my story.

'That's sad,' he said. 'But you have learnt, like me, that one owner isn't always enough. I visit another house on my street sometimes.'

'Really?' I said, intrigued.

'I think of myself as being a doorstep cat,' he said.

'What's that?' I was curious.

'Well, you live somewhere most of the time, but you go to other doorsteps until they let you in. They don't always, but I have another house, and although I don't stay there, if anything happens I feel I have options.' As I questioned him he went on to explain that a doorstep cat got fed multiple times, by multiple families, they got petted and fussed over and enjoyed a high level of security.

Like me he had hated being homeless; and unlike me the young child had come to his rescue although he said that he'd engineered it. When he found his new family he'd looked as helpless as possible, ensuring they took pity and adopted him.

'So you just looked like you needed feeding and grooming?' I asked, ears pricked in interest.

'Well I really did look like that. But you know, I got lucky, I pleaded for help and someone took me in. I'll help you if you like.'

'Oh I would love that,' I replied.

He let me curl up with him in his basket, talking late into the night. And although I wouldn't get much sleep, because I needed to leave early the next morning before Button's owners woke, I felt safe for the first time since leaving Margaret's. I also had a plan forming in my mind: I would make an excellent doorstep cat.

# Chapter
# Five

I left Button's house the next morning. I felt sad about going, after the safety of the night, but at least he'd advised me where to go, pointing me in the direction of the nicer streets in the area. He suggested I head west, towards the area that was popular with families, until I found the street that felt right to me. I had to trust my instincts and he seemed to think I would know when I had arrived. With a good sleep and a full belly I headed off in the direction he'd suggested, dodging danger and following my nose.

I was more optimistic but life after Button didn't suddenly change overnight. There were still days where I had to keep my wits about me and more still where I felt hungry and tired, having to keep going when my legs shook with exhaustion and my fur stuck to my body with the rain. I survived but it was a long, hard journey. I just kept telling myself it would be worth it in the end.

And, finally I arrived at a lovely street and as Button had suggested, I knew immediately it would give me what I needed. I didn't know how exactly, but I knew; I just knew, that I belonged here. I sat by a sign that said 'Edgar Road' and I licked my lips. For the first time since leaving Margaret's, I felt that everything was going to be all right.

I immediately liked Edgar Road. It was a long street with many different types of houses; Victorian terraced houses, modern boxes, larger houses and some buildings divided into flats. What I especially liked was that there were a number of 'For Sale' and 'To Let' signs. Button had explained that these signs meant that new people would soon be arriving. And, I strongly believed, what new people needed most of all, was a cat like me.

In the next few days, I met some of the neighbourhood cats. When I told them what I was up to, they insisted on helping me. I soon discovered that, on the whole, the Edgar Road cats were a pretty nice bunch. After all, it was important to me to live in a neighbourhood with good cat neighbours. There were a couple of 'Alpha Toms' and one pretty girl cat who was particularly unkind to everyone, but apart from that they were friendly, and they shared their food and drink with me when I was at my most needy.

During the day I spent my time speaking to the other cats, getting as much information as I could out of them, and casing out the empty houses, searching for my potential homes. At night, I would go hunting, just to keep myself fed.

One evening, after I'd been at Edgar Road for just under a week, a particularly mean Tom found me sitting outside one of the empty houses that I was keeping an eye on.

'You don't live here. Maybe it's time you left,' he hissed at me.

'I'm staying,' I hissed back, trying to be brave as I faced him. He was bigger than me and of course, I was still not at my best. After all I'd been through, I felt as if I had no more fight inside me but I couldn't give up. I was suddenly distracted by a noise, and I looked up to see a bird swooping quite low overhead. The Tom took his chance and swiped at me with his paw, scratching me just above my eye.

I yowled. It really hurt and I quickly felt blood. I spat at the Tom as he loomed in, looking as if he was going to bite me. I vowed to always keep my eye on him in future.

A brightly striped cat called Tiger lived next door to this empty house, and she and I had become friendly. She suddenly appeared, and stood between me and the Tom.

'Get lost, Bandit,' she hissed. Bandit looked as though he might fight, but after a while, he turned on his heel and stalked off. 'You're bleeding,' she said.

'He caught me unawares, I was distracted,' I said, haughtily. 'I could have taken him easily.' Tiger grinned.

'Look Alfie, I am sure you could, but you're still delicate. Anyway, come with me and I'll sneak you some food.'

As I followed her, I knew she would be my best cat friend on the street.


'You don't look very good,' Tiger commented as I was gratefully eating. I tried not to feel affronted.

'I know,' I replied, sadly. It was true. By the time I arrived in Edgar Road I was thinner than I had ever been. My fur was certainly no longer shiny and I was tired from living outside and from malnourishment. I had no idea how long it had taken me to get there, but it felt like a long time. The weather had changed; it was getting warmer and the nights were lighter. It felt as if the sun was getting ready to come out.

As I became friends with Tiger, I was also becoming accustomed to my new road. I had prowled extensively, so I knew the street as well as the back of my paw. I knew where every cat lived and if they were nice or not. I knew where the mean dogs were, and after a fair few escapes from such dogs, I knew which houses to avoid at all costs. I had balanced on every fence and wall in Edgar Road. I knew it as my new home, or homes, to be more accurate.

# Chapter
# Six

I sat and watched as two burly men unloaded the last of the furniture from the removal van. I was, so far, pleased with what I had seen: a comfortable looking blue sofa; large floor cushions; a fancy upholstered armchair which looked as if it might be an antique, not that I was an expert. I had seen lots more being taken off the van; wardrobes, chests of drawers and lots of sealed boxes, but I was mostly interested in soft furnishings.

Flicking my tail in satisfaction, I felt my whiskers rising as I grinned. It looked as if I had found my first potential new home; 78 Edgar Road.

While the removals men took a break and were drinking out of plastic flask cups, I seized the opportunity to sneak into the house. Despite my curiosity, I first made my way straight through to check out the back door. Although I had been in all of the gardens in the street, and felt confident that this house did, in fact, possess a cat flap, I still needed to be sure. It did. I purred with pleasure at my cleverness and slid through it, deciding to hide out in the garden.

After chasing my shadow around in the tiny garden, and looking for flies to torment, I shivered with excitement and decided to groom myself thoroughly one last time. I was brimming with expectation as I made my way back into the house and anticipated how nice it would be to be a domestic cat again. How I yearned for a lap to sit on, milk to be given to me and food aplenty. Simple needs but, as I had learnt, not needs to be taken for granted. Nothing could ever be taken for granted again.

I wasn't a silly cat. My journey, and those I'd met along the way, had taught me many things. There was no way I was going to put all my whiskers in one basket ever again. It was a lesson I'd learnt the hard way. The worst way. Some of my peers were either too trusting or too lazy, but I had discovered that I couldn't afford to be either. As much as I wanted to be a loyal cat with a loyal owner, it was just too precarious. I couldn't ever be in the situation I was in before. I couldn't bear to be alone ever again.

I felt my fur stand on end as I pushed the terror of the past weeks out of my head and instead turned my attention to my new owner. I hoped that they would be as nice as their soft furnishings.

As I padded around the house I noticed the sky begin to turn dusky and I sensed the temperature drop. I wondered why someone would move their furniture into the house, but not themselves; it didn't make sense. I started to feel a little panicked for the owner I hadn't yet met. But then I told myself to relax and gave my whiskers a lick to calm myself down. I needed to look my best for when the people arrived at their new home; I was getting far too anxious.

The problem was that I had spent too long as a homeless cat, and I couldn't face it any more. Just as I felt as if I might start fretting again, I heard the front door open. I immediately pricked up my ears and stretched out my body. It was time to go and meet my first new family. I plastered my most charming smile on my face.

'I know Mum, but I couldn't help it,' I heard a female voice say. There was a pause. 'I couldn't be here because the blasted car broke down just two hours into the journey and I have just spent the last three hours with a very talkative RAC man, who, quite frankly, nearly sent me mad.' Another pause. Her voice sounded nice although she was clearly exasperated, I thought, as I crept nearer. 'They did. It looks like all the furniture is here, and, as I asked, the keys were posted through the front door.' Pause. 'Edgar Road isn't the ghetto, Mum, I think it'll be fine. Anyway, I've just walked through the door to my new home after the day from hell, so I'll call you tomorrow.'

I rounded the corner and came face to face with a woman. She looked fairly young, although I wasn't very good at judging age; all I could say was that her face wasn't full of wrinkles, like Margaret's. She was quite tall, very thin and had untidy dark-blonde hair and sad blue eyes. My first impression of her was that she gave me a nice feeling, and her sad eyes drew me to her strongly. My cat's instinct told me that she needed me as much as I needed her. I, like most cats, didn't judge humans on appearance; we read personality, and normally cats have a special talent for knowing who is good and who is bad. 'She'll do nicely,' I immediately thought feeling pleased.

'Who are you?' she said, her voice suddenly soft; the type of voice so many people reserve for pets and babies as if we are stupid. I would have given her a disdainful look, but I needed to be charming. So instead I gave her one of my best grins. She knelt down beside me and I purred, moving slowly towards her, gently brushing her leg. Oh yes, I knew how to flirt when I needed to.

'You poor thing, you look half starved. And your fur, it's all patchy, as if you've been fighting. Have you been fighting?' She sounded very tender and I purred in agreement. I had only seen my reflection in water lately but I knew from Tiger that I didn't look my best. I just hoped that it didn't put her off as I nestled into her legs again.

'Oh, you are sweet. What's your name?' She looked at the silver disc hanging from my neck. 'Alfie. Well, hello, Alfie.' She gently picked me up and stroked my 'patchy' fur. It felt heavenly after all this time. I felt as if I was bonding with the lady, learning her smell, transferring mine and reminding me of my past, my kittenhood. I felt myself relax in a way I had only dreamt of recently.

Once again I purred my best purr and snuggled into her. 'Well, Alfie, I'm Claire and although I'm pretty sure a cat didn't come with the house, let's find you something to eat. I'll call your owner in a bit.' I grinned again. She could try all she wanted, but the number on the disc wouldn't work. I triumphantly strode next to her, tail upright, my way of saying a proper 'hello' to my new friend, as she went back to the front door, picked up two carrier bags and carried them into the kitchen.

As she unpacked her shopping, I looked properly at my new feeding area. The kitchen was small but modern. It had white shiny units and wooden work surfaces. It was clean and uncluttered. Mind you, I reminded myself, no one lived here properly yet. In my old house, which it still pained me to think of, the kitchen had been very old fashioned and cluttered. It was dominated by a huge sideboard and there were decorative plates everywhere. I accidentally broke one when I was very young. Margaret had been so upset that I didn't go near them again. However, I doubted that Claire had any decorative plates. She didn't look the type.

'Here you go,' she said triumphantly, laying down a bowl that she had unpacked and poured some milk into. She then opened a packet and laid some smoked salmon on a plate. 'Oh, what a glorious welcome,' I thought. Obviously I hadn't expected her to have cat food, but at the same time I hadn't imagined getting such a treat. I would have been happy with anything today, even just milk. I decided there and then that I liked Claire. As I ate, she picked a glass out of the same box that had contained the bowl and pulled a bottle of wine out of the carrier bag. She poured a glass, drank it greedily and then poured another. I raised my eyes in surprise. She must have been very thirsty.

I finished eating, and rubbed against Claire's legs in thanks. She seemed a bit lost but then she looked at me.

'Oh dear, I need to call your owners,' she said, as if she'd forgotten. I miaowed to tell her I didn't have any, but she didn't seem to understand. She crouched down and looked at my silver disc. She punched the numbers into her phone and waited. Although I knew no one would answer, I still felt nervous. 'That's odd,' she said. 'The phone line is dead; there must be a fault. Don't worry, I'm not going to kick you out. Stay here tonight and I'll try again tomorrow.'

I purred very loudly in thanks, and felt immensely relieved.

'But, if you're going to stay for the night, you need a bath,' she said, picking me up. I pricked up my ears in horror. A bath? I was a cat, I bathed myself. I cried, as if to object. 'Sorry, Alfie, but you smell terrible,' she added. 'Now, I'll just go and unpack some towels and then we'll sort you out.'

I resisted the urge to jump out of her arms and run away again. I hated water and I knew what a bath meant, having had one at Margaret's a long time ago when I came home covered in mud. It was an awful experience, although, I reasoned, not as bad as being homeless, so I decided to once again be a brave cat.

She put me in front of a big mirror in her bedroom while she went to find the towels. I looked and I yelped in surprise.

If I didn't know better, I would have thought that I was looking at another animal; I looked even worse than I had initially felt. My fur was patchy, I looked so thin that I could see my bones poking through and despite my best efforts at cleaning myself, Claire was right, I looked dirty. I felt suddenly sad; it seemed that since Margaret's death I had changed both inside and out.

Claire fetched me and took me to the bathroom where she ran the water and then put me gently in the bath. I screeched and wriggled a bit.

'Sorry, Alfie, but you need a good wash.' She looked a bit confused as she held a bottle in one of her hands. 'It's natural shampoo so it should be OK. Oh God, I don't know, I've never had a cat before.' She looked a bit upset. 'And you're not my cat. I hope your owner isn't too worried.' I saw a tear escape out of her eye. 'This isn't what was supposed to happen.' I wanted to comfort her; she clearly needed it, but I couldn't because I was still in the bath and I felt like I resembled a giant soap sud.

After the bath, which seemed to go on forever, she wrapped me in a towel and dried me off.

When I finally felt dry again, I followed Claire to the living room, where she slumped onto the newly delivered sofa and I jumped up next to her. It was every bit as comfortable as I had hoped, and she didn't tell me off or try to push me down. Like polite strangers, I sat on one side, she on the other. She picked up her glass, took a smaller sip, and sighed. I studied her as she looked around the room as if seeing it for the first time. There were boxes that needed unpacking, a television that sat in the middle of the room and a small dining table and chairs tucked into a corner. Apart from the sofa, it wasn't organised and it wasn't really home yet. As if Claire had read my thoughts, she took another sip of her drink and then she burst into tears.

'What the hell have I done?' she said, crying noisily.

Despite the noise, I was upset at how distraught she had suddenly become, but I knew what I had to do. It was as if there was a reason I was here now; I felt a sense of purpose. Perhaps I could help Claire as much as she could help me? I moved across the sofa and nestled into her, laying my little head gently on her lap. She automatically stroked me, and although she was still crying, I was offering her the comfort that I somehow knew she needed and she was doing the same for me. You see, I understood, because at that moment I knew with certainty in my heart that we were kindred spirits.

I had come home again.

# Chapter Seven

chapter
seven

It had been a week since I'd been living with Claire and we had settled into quite a comfortable routine, although not an entirely healthy one. She cried a lot and I snuggled a lot, which suited me just fine. I loved to cuddle, and I had a lot of lost time to make up for. I just wished I could do something to stop Claire from crying so much. It was clear that she needed my help and I vowed I would give it in any way I could.

Claire had tried to phone the number on my disc again, then she'd phoned the telephone company and discovered it had been disconnected. She assumed I'd been abandoned, and that seemed to make her like me even more. She cried over it and said that she couldn't understand how anyone could do that to me. She also said that she totally understood, as it had happened to her, although I was yet to discover the details. But I knew that I had a home with her. She started buying me cat food and special milk. She got me a litter tray, not that I really liked using them, and she was talking, luckily only talking, about taking me to the vet. Vets tended to poke around where they were not wanted, but she hadn't called them so far, so paws crossed she'd forget about that.

Despite the almost constant crying, Claire was very efficient. She managed to get all her furniture arranged and her boxes unpacked in only a couple of days. She organised the house and it quickly looked like a home. Pictures were hung on the walls, cushions scattered literally everywhere, and suddenly warmth flooded into every room; I had chosen well.

However, as I said, it wasn't a happy home. Claire had been unpacking and I had watched her, trying my best to work out her story. She arranged lots of photographs in the front room, telling me who was in them; her mum and dad, pictures of herself as a child, her younger brother, friends and extended family. For a while she was animated and happy, and I rewarded her positivity by brushing up against her legs the way she told me she liked. I did this a lot for her; after all, I needed her to love me so I wouldn't have to go back to the streets again. I needed to love her, too, although I was finding this increasingly easy to do.

One evening, she unpacked a photo which she didn't tell me about. It was a picture of her in a white dress, holding hands with a man who looked very smart. I'd learnt enough about humans to know that this was what they called a 'wedding photo', when two people joined together and said they would only mate with each other – something this cat certainly didn't understand. She sank into the sofa, clutching the photo against her chest, and started sobbing loudly. I sat next to her, giving her my equivalent of a cry, which was a loud yowl, but she didn't seem to take any notice of me. But then I started yowling in earnest; like Claire, I couldn't stop, as my loss flooded my memory. Although I didn't know if the man in the suit had left her, or died the way my Margaret had, I knew then that she really was on her own. Just as I had been. We sat side by side, her crying, me yowling, at the top of our voices.

After a couple more days, Claire left early in the morning, saying that she had to go to work. She looked a bit better, as she put on a smart outfit and brushed her hair. She even had some colour to her face, although I wasn't sure it was exactly natural. I was also beginning to look better, even in a few short days. My fur was beginning to even out a bit and I was putting on weight again, now that I was eating so much and exercising so little. As we stood side by side, looking in Claire's big mirror, I thought we made a very cute couple. Or we had the potential to be, at the very least.

But although Claire left food for me, I missed her company when she was at work and felt sad to be alone again. I had Tiger of course and we spent time together, our friendship growing as we chased flies, went for short strolls and basked in the sun in her back garden, but that was my cat friendship; I knew that more than anything now I needed humans I could rely on.

When Claire was out at work, it brought back unwelcome memories and made me think that it was time to carry on with my plan. If I was going to ensure that I was never on my own again, I would need more than one home. That was the sad fact of life.

I'd seen a 'Sold' sign go up outside number 46, at about the same time that one had been erected outside Claire's house and I'd been scoping both, but of course Claire had arrived first. However, I'd noticed that 46 was now also occupied. This house was just far enough apart from Claire's to give me a short walk. It was on the part of the road that had the larger houses – the 'posh' bit, as I had been told by the cats that lived here and who seemed very proud and a little bit boastful of the fact. It looked like it would be a good place to live too, for at least part of the time.

Edgar Road was an unusual road; because of the different types of houses, there was a real difference in the types of people who lived there. The house I had lived in with

Margaret, the only house I had ever known, was a small house on a very tiny street – completely different to some of the huge houses that lined the far end of the road.

Claire's house was medium sized, and this house – number 46 – was among the best. It was bigger than Claire's house; taller and wider, and the windows were large and imposing. I could imagine myself sitting on a windowsill looking out of one of them quite happily. As it was a big house, I assumed that a family would be living there and I quite liked the idea of being a family cat too. Now, don't get me wrong, I liked Claire very much and had grown extremely fond of her. I had no intention of abandoning her, but I needed to have more than one home – just to make sure I didn't end up alone again.

It was dawn when I turned my attention to number 46. A very slick car with only two seats was parked outside, which worried me, as that didn't seem to be appropriate for a family. But still, I had already made my decision, so I wanted to investigate further. I made my way round to the back of the house where I found, to my delight, that there was a cat flap waiting for me.

I found myself in a very smart room with a washing machine, dryer and huge fridge freezer. It loomed over me, like a giant, making a loud humming noise that hurt my ears. I pushed through an open door and walked into an enormous kitchen, which was dominated by a large dining table. I felt as if I'd struck gold; a table that big would definitely need lots of children around it, and everyone knew that children loved cats. I'd be spoilt. I felt my excitement grow; I really wanted to be spoilt.

Just as I was dreaming of all the food, games and cuddles I'd get, a woman and a man entered the room.

'I didn't know you had a cat,' she said, screeching slightly. The pitch of her voice was quite high, a bit like a mouse. I was disappointed to see that she didn't look at all motherly; she wore a very tight dress with shoes that were almost higher than me. I wondered how on earth she managed to breathe or walk. She also looked like she hadn't seen any grooming in a while. Now, I'm not a judgemental cat as a general rule, but I pride myself on always taking care of my appearance. I started to clean my paws and lick down my fur in the hope that she'd take the hint.

Her voice was like the woman in one of the soap operas I used to watch with Margaret. *EastEnders*, I think it was called.

I blinked at the man to say 'hello' but he didn't blink back.

'I don't,' he replied in a cold voice. I looked at him. He was tall with dark hair and quite a handsome face, but he didn't look very friendly and as he looked me over, he began to seem a bit cross.

'I moved in a couple of days ago and only just noticed that there's a bloody cat flap which I'll have to block up before all the scraggy neighbourhood cats take up residence here.' He glared at me, as if to convey that he was talking about me. I shrank into myself defensively.

I couldn't believe my ears. This man was horrible and it was a huge disappointment that there were no children around. There were no toys in the kitchen anyway, and these two didn't seem to be capable of looking after a cat or a child. It looked as if I had got it very wrong. So much for a cat's intuition.

'Oh, Jonathan,' the lady said. 'Don't be so mean. He's a cute little thing. And he might be hungry.' I instantly regretted my unkind thoughts; this lady might look like a mess but she was kind. My hope began to rise.

'I know very little about cats and I don't care to know more,' he replied, sounding haughty. 'But I do know that if you give them food they'll come back, so let's not go there. Anyway, I have work to do. I'll show you out.'

The woman looked as upset as I felt, as Jonathan led her to the door. I curled myself up, trying to look my youngest and cutest for his return. But instead of melting, as I expected, he picked me up and threw – literally, threw – me out of the front door. I landed on my feet, so luckily I was unhurt.

'New house, new start, not a new bloody cat,' he said, as he slammed the door in my face.

I shook myself off, mortally offended. How dare that man treat me like that? I also felt sorry for the woman he threw out. I hoped he hadn't manhandled her in the same way.

I suppose that should have been the end of my attempt to make a home out of number 46, but then, I'm not a cat to give up easily. I couldn't believe that the man, Jonathan, was as horrible as he seemed. Using my cat senses, I got the feeling that he was more miserable than mean. After all, when the lady left, he was clearly alone, and I knew all about how hideous that could be.

I rushed back to Claire's to see her before she went to work. I could tell she'd been crying, because she was putting lots of stuff on her face to hide it. When she'd finished making herself look nice (which took her much longer than it took me), she fed and petted me, before grabbing her bag and leaving the house again. I walked her to the door, rubbing myself against her legs, purring and trying to convey that I was there for her.

And wishing that there was more I could do to make her feel better.

'Alfie, what would I do without you?' she rewarded me by saying, before she left. I preened myself. After being horribly rejected by Jonathan, it was nice to be appreciated. I was falling in love with this sad young lady that I somehow knew I needed to help. People accuse us cats of being self-centred and egotistical but that is often far from the case. I was a cat who wanted to aid those in need. I was a kind, loving type of cat with a very special new mission to help people.

I should have left Jonathan and number 46 alone, but something drew me back. My Margaret used to say that angry people were really just unhappy people, and she was the wisest person I'd ever met. When I first moved in with her, Agnes was very angry and Margaret said that it was because she was worried I would take her place. Agnes confirmed this, when she thawed towards me. I learnt then that anger and unhappiness were fine basket mates.

So I returned to number 46. The car was absent from the front so the coast was clear. Feeling brave, I went through the cat flap and took a look around. I'd been right, the house was big and looked as if it should contain a family but, on closer inspection, it was a manly space. There were no soft touches, no floral patterns, no pink. It was all gleaming surfaces, glass and chrome. His sofa was the sort that I'd seen in some of the smart looking furniture shop windows I'd passed on my travels; metal and cream, which would never suit children – or cats, for that matter. I walked across the sofa, back and forth a few times, feeling satisfied. My paws were clean though, so I wasn't being that naughty – I just wanted to test it out. I made my way upstairs, where I found four bedrooms; two had beds, one was an office, and the last was full of boxes. This house had no personal touches. No happy photos, nothing to suggest that anyone lived there apart from the furniture. It seemed as cold as the big, scary fridge freezer.

I decided that this Jonathan man would be something of a challenge. After fending for myself for so long, I knew what I was capable of. This man clearly didn't like me, or any cat for that matter, but that wasn't a new experience for me. As I thought of Agnes again, her near-black face popped into my head and made me smile. I missed her so much, it was like there was a part of me missing.

Agnes was the opposite to me in every way; a very gentle old cat. She would spend most of her time sitting in the window on a special cushion watching the world go by.

When I arrived, a playful bundle of fluff, she immediately took umbrage.

'If you think you're staying in my house, you can think again,' she hissed at me when we first met. She tried to attack me a couple of times but I was too fast for her, and Margaret would chastise her before making even more of a fuss of me, giving me treats and buying me toys. After a while, Agnes decided that she would reluctantly accept me as long as I didn't bother her, and slowly, I charmed her and won her round. By the time the vet said that she had to go to cat heaven, we were family and we loved each other. I felt a physical pain as I remembered how Agnes would groom me, just as my mother had done when I was born.

If I could get around the intimidating Agnes, then surely Jonathan would be cat's play?

After stalking round his house wondering what he would do with all that space, I decided that I would go out and get him a gift. Despite the fact that hunting wasn't my favourite pastime, I wanted to make friends with him and this was the only way I knew how.

My cat comrades from my time on the streets had given me mixed messages. Some of them took their gifts in constantly, despite the fact that at times, it made their owners angry. Others, like me, were smarter about when it was appropriate. It was, after all, our way of showing we cared. And I presumed that Jonathan was a man who liked to hunt, he seemed quite like an Alpha Tom, so I was pretty sure he would appreciate a gift. It would show him that we had something in common.

I called for Tiger and asked if she wanted to join me.

'I was sleeping. Why can't you be a normal cat and hunt at night?' she sighed, although she reluctantly agreed to come with me.

She was right, cats normally hunted at night, but in my time on the streets I had learnt that it was also possible to find prey during the day which was my preference. I started prowling, and it didn't take long for me to locate a juicy mouse. I crouched down low ready to pounce and then I quickly went in for the kill. The mouse ran one way then the other so I had difficulty trapping it with my paw. I flicked this way and that as it continued to elude me.

'You are such a terrible hunter,' Tiger laughed as she stood back watching.

'You could help me,' I hissed but she laughed again. Finally, just before I ran out of patience the mouse ran out of energy. I pounced again and at last I had it in my paws.

'Do you want to come with me to take it to Jonathan's?' I asked.

'Yes, I want to see your second home,' Tiger replied.

I decided that as I wanted Jonathan to like me, I wouldn't decapitate the mouse, and so I carefully carried it in my mouth through the cat flap. I deposited it by the front door, so there was no way that he could miss it. I briefly wished that I could write, because if I could, I'd leave a note saying, 'Welcome to your new home,' but instead I could only hope he would get my lovely message.

# Chapter
# Eight

chapter
eight

I was late getting back to number 78, because Tiger and I had been lurking in the bushes, playing with falling leaves and waiting for Jonathan to get back. But as it got later, the sky began to darken and I started to get hungry. Due to my sacrifice of the mouse, I hadn't eaten since breakfast so, reluctantly, I made my way back to Claire.

I let myself in through the cat flap and found her in the kitchen.

'Hello, Alfie,' she said, bending down to give me a stroke. 'Where have you been today? she asked. I replied with a purr. She reached into the cupboard and brought down a tin of cat food. She opened a carton of special cat milk.

'Don't mind if I do,' I thought, as I tucked in. When I'd eaten, I cleaned my whiskers thoroughly, while I watched Claire tidy up. I was learning more about Claire every day. Despite the fact that she seemed depressed, she was also very clean and tidy – that explained my horrible bath. She wouldn't even leave an empty glass on the side in the kitchen. Everything was washed up, and put away. She was the same with her clothes. The house was immaculate, and she cleaned all surfaces frequently. More than was necessary, I thought. She had bought me special bowls to eat from and she'd place them on the floor for me, but when I'd finished dining, she would scoop them up and clean them immediately, and then she would spray and clean the floor. I was a pretty fastidious cat when it came to personal hygiene, but being with Claire made me clean myself more than usual; I didn't want her to think I wasn't worthy of her spotless house. And I especially didn't want another bath.

Every day when she got back from work, which she had told me was in a big office, doing something called 'Marketing', she would shower – she was always moaning about the dirt in London – then she would change into pyjamas, pour herself something to drink, and go and sit on the sofa. She would then normally start to cry. It had become a set routine in the short time that I'd been here.

She did eat, but very little, and I couldn't help but notice that she was really quite bony, the way I had been when I'd first arrived here. I knew I needed to try to get her to eat more food but I had no idea how. She seemed to drink quite a lot from a fancy glass, though. She always kept a bottle of wine in the fridge and she would empty it almost nightly. It made me think of the homeless people who had threatened to eat me. I know she wasn't like them, but Button had explained the human concept of being drunk and I think Claire spent most nights a little bit so. After all, it was usually after a couple of these drinks that she would start crying. And although I would always comfort her when she did this, whatever I did, I couldn't get her to stop. It made me sad, because all I wanted to do was to make her smile or at least put a stop to her tears.

So far, I had tried playing 'hiding behind the curtains', to make her laugh, but she had acted as if I was invisible. I even fell off the windowsill once in my attempt to cheer her up and she didn't notice that either, despite the fact that I yelped in pain. I tried crying with her; purring, nuzzling into her with my little warm head, giving her my precious tail to play with, but to no end. When she got very sad she would shut everything out, including me.

At night, when she went to bed, I would go and sleep on an armchair next to her. She put a blanket on it for me, so it was perfectly comfortable, and it meant I could keep an eye on her. I would doze a bit but for most of the night I would watch her sleep, trying to make her feel that she wasn't on her own. When her alarm went off in the morning, I would gently jump on her and lick her nose. I wanted her to feel loved when she opened her eyes every day, just as I did.

But still, I felt sad myself, sometimes. Worrying about Claire was emotionally tiring, but I hoped that if I just stuck to my plan to help her, somehow I would know what to do; the answers had to be there somewhere.

We had just gone into the sitting room that evening; her with her glass, me with my catnip toy that she had kindly bought me, when the doorbell rang. She looked a bit surprised as she went to open the door. I followed her protectively, touching her legs as she walked. A man stood on her doorstep. At first, I wondered if it was the man from the photo, but on closer inspection it wasn't, although I did recognise him from some of the pictures. It was Tim, Claire's brother. She didn't look very happy to see him, though.

'Didn't take long for you to embrace the cliché,' he said.

'What are you talking about?' she snapped.

'Single women and cats. Sorry Claire, only joking.' He smiled, but she did not and neither did I; we both stood aside and let him in. We followed him into the living room.

'What are you doing here, Tim?' she asked, as she gestured for him to sit down. I stayed by her side.

'Can't I visit my sister?' he replied. He tried to stroke me but I arched myself away from him; I wasn't sure if he was friend or foe. 'Who's this?' he asked.

'Alfie, he came with the house. Anyway, why didn't you tell me you were coming? It's not as if you could have been just passing.'

'I'm only an hour and a half away, Claire, and it was a spur of the moment thing.'

Claire seemed to be scrutinising him as she sat down in an armchair. I jumped onto her lap, trying to give Tim a haughty look, although I'm not sure I pulled it off. Sometimes it's hard being as cute as me; people and cats don't take me seriously.

'Why didn't you call me, at least?' she pushed.

'OK, let's cut to the chase. I'm guessing you're not going to offer me a drink?' he asked. She shook her head resolutely.

'Mum asked me to come. She's worried about you. You know, it's only been six months since Steve left you. You sell up and move a four-hour drive away from your home and Mum and Dad; from your friends and your job, to London – not exactly a friendly city – where you've never lived, and don't know anyone. Of course we're worried. Worried sick. And Mum is beside herself.'

'Well you can stop worrying. Look at me, I'm fine.' She looked and sounded angry.

'Claire, I *am* looking at you, and you seem anything but fine.'

Claire sighed. 'Tim, I needed to get away, can't you try to understand? Steve left me for another woman and they live down the road from my old house, not to mention near Mum and Dad. I couldn't bear to see them every day, which I would have done if I'd stayed. I think you should all be proud of me. I gave him the quick divorce he wanted. I didn't make a fuss. I sold our home, got myself a really good job, and bought this house. I did all that while my heart was broken into a thousand pieces.' She stopped and wiped the tears from her cheek. I nestled into her as much as I could.

'And that is great, Claire,' Tim sounded softer too. 'But we're worried about how you really are. You've done amazingly, but you're unhappy and Mum feels that you're too far away. Can you just do me a favour and go home for the weekend soon, just to reassure her?'

I thought that it might be a good idea; Claire would see her family and it would give me a chance to explore further, without having to worry about her. Was I being selfish? I hoped not.

'Listen, Tim, I'll make a deal. I'll go home one weekend if you promise to tell Mum that I seem all right to you.'

'OK Sis, I'll do that, but you know what? Can you at least make me a cup of tea before I start the long drive back?'

I decided to make friends with Tim when I realised he was an ally for Claire. We played with some of my toys together and I liked the way he got down on his hands and knees to fuss me, not minding that he looked daft. I rolled on my back, with my legs in the air and let him tickle my tummy; one of my favourite things ever. And while we played, he asked me to look after his sister and I tried to convey to him that I definitely would. I felt the weight of responsibility but I was ready for it. After we waved him off, I wondered if I could sneak out and go and see if Jonathan was home, but instead, Claire picked me up and carried me up to bed.

# Chapter
# Nine

I arrived again at number 46 when it was barely light. Claire had told me that she had an early start at work and although she took the time to leave me some food, she rushed out of the door without giving me any affection. I tried not to be offended; humans were like that, they had a lot more stuff going on than we cats did. But still, it reinforced my view that I needed more people to look after me.

I let myself in through the cat flap. The house was so quiet, almost eerie. It was also in darkness all the curtains were drawn and the blinds down. Being largely nocturnal animals, we cats are very good at seeing in the dark and using our other senses to negotiate our way around. I was quite an expert at dodging both indoor dangers, like furniture, and outdoor ones, like trees and other animals.

I wondered for a moment what it would be like, being Jonathan. Having this big space, but being in it alone. That made no sense to me. In my cat basket in my old house, I would curl into the side, making myself as cosy as possible. If I'd had a basket that was any bigger, it wouldn't have felt like home. Actually, my favourite times were after Agnes thawed towards me and we shared a basket. The warmth and the comfort that I got from her was wonderful. I missed it every day of my life. I wondered if Jonathan felt the same, and whether that was why the woman had been in his house yesterday. Did they snuggle like Agnes and I did? I thought they probably did. Although, if he wasn't nicer to her, I doubted she would come back.

I sat in the hallway at the bottom of the staircase. One of the many things wrong with Jonathan's house was his lack of carpet. Every floor was wooden, which could be quite a lot of fun for a cat – I had already discovered the joy of sliding along the floor on my bottom – but it was cold, and I loved a carpet to scratch at. And instead of curtains to play with, he had these rigid things which weren't any fun. I realised, yet again, that this wasn't really a house meant for a cat, but I still couldn't help but be drawn to it.

After what seemed like ages, a dishevelled Jonathan appeared on the stairs, still wearing his pyjamas. He looked tired and scruffy; a bit like I did before a good groom. He stopped and stared straight at me, but he didn't exactly look pleased to see me.

'Please tell me you didn't leave the dead mouse on my mat?' he said crossly.

I gave him my best purr, as if to say, 'You're welcome.'

'You bloody cat. I thought I told you that you weren't wanted here.' He looked and sounded angry as he pushed past me into the kitchen. He took a mug out of the cupboard and started pressing buttons on a machine. I watched as coffee poured into the cup. He went to the fridge, which looked like a spaceship, and pulled out some milk. As he poured some into his mug I licked my lips hopefully. He ignored me, so I let out my loudest miaow.

'If you think I'm giving you milk, you've got another think coming,' he snapped.

Honestly, he really was playing hard to get. I miaowed again to convey my disapproval.

'I don't need a pet,' he continued, as he sipped his drink. 'I need peace and quiet, to try to get my life here sorted out.' I pricked my ears to show I was interested. 'I don't need dead mice on my doorstep, thank you very much, and I don't need anyone disrupting my peace.'

I purred again, this time in an effort to win him round a bit.

'It's bad enough being in this bloody cold country again.' He looked at me as if he was speaking to a human. If I could have, I would have told him that it wasn't that cold, after all, it was summer. He continued. 'I miss Singapore. I miss the heat and I miss the lifestyle. I made one mistake and that was that. Back here. No job, no girlfriend.' He paused to take another sip of his drink. My eyes narrowed as he began to open up. 'Oh yes, she left me soon enough when I lost my job. Three years of paying for everything for her and she couldn't even console me for one day before she buggered off. And yes, I was lucky that I had enough money to buy this house, but let's face it, it's hardly bloody Chelsea, is it?' I didn't exactly know what 'Chelsea' was, but I tried to look as if I agreed with him.

I felt happy as I flicked my tail up in triumph. I was right; he was sad and lonely and not just a grumpy man, although he *was* undoubtedly grumpy. But I saw an opportunity; a small one, but one all the same. Jonathan needed a friend, and this cat made an excellent friend.

'And why am I talking to a bloody cat? It's not as if you even understand.' How little he knew, I thought, as he drank the rest of his coffee. To show that I did indeed understand, I rubbed up against his legs, giving him the affection that I knew he craved. He looked surprised but he didn't immediately pull away. I decided to push my luck, so I jumped up onto his lap. He looked surprised. However, just as he looked like he would soften, he bristled.

'Right, I am going to phone your owner and tell them that

you need collecting,' he said, angrily. He gently took hold of my disc and then he did what Claire had done and dialled the number. When the number didn't work, he tutted and looked annoyed.

'Where the hell do you live?' I tilted my head at him. 'Look, you need to go home. I can't stand around all day dealing with you. I've got a job to find and a cat flap to get removed.' He looked at me with mean eyes before walking away.

I felt happier, though. Firstly, he had started talking to me, which was a very good sign, and secondly, he hadn't thrown me out. He had walked away knowing I was still in his house. Maybe he was growing to like me. I really thought this man might have a bark worse than his bite.

I tentatively followed him upstairs, but kept out of the way as I looked around. I wanted to learn more about him, so I thought observing him would be a good idea.

He was a tall man, and not fat at all. I prided myself on my appearance and, by the looks of it, Jonathan did, too. We definitely had something in common there. He took a very long shower in a room which was attached to his bedroom, and when he came out, he opened a long built-in wardrobe and picked out a suit. When dressed, he looked smart, like one of those men in the old black and white films my Margaret used to love. She said they were 'suave and handsome, just as men should be', and I have to say, I think she would have approved of Jonathan's looks.

Quietly I made my way downstairs, careful that he hadn't seen me watching him, and I waited again, at the bottom of the stairs.

'You still here, Alfie?' he said, but he didn't sound quite as hostile as before.

I miaowed in reply. He shook his head but I felt warm inside; he had used my name!

He went to the cupboard under the stairs, where there was a row of black shiny shoes, and picked out a pair. He sat on the stairs to put them on. Then he pulled a jacket off the coat rack and took his keys from the console table in the hall.

'Right, Alfie, I guess you can show yourself out this time, and please don't let me find you here when I get back. Or any more dead things.' As he shut the door behind me, I stretched my legs in pleasure. I knew now that I could help Jonathan. He was sad, angry and lonely and, like Claire, he really needed me. He just might not have realised it yet.

He was softening, and so quickly. I thought about what I could do to win him over, and I realised that despite what he said, he needed another present. But not a mouse this time, something a bit prettier. A bird! That was it, I would bring him a bird. After all, nothing says 'let's be friends' like a dead bird.

Later that afternoon, I deposited the bird on the doormat as I had done with the mouse. Surely now Jonathan would understand that I wanted to be his friend. I felt quite happy, so I decided to take a walk to the end of the street, basking in the sunshine. It wasn't exactly hot, but it was a nice day and if you found the right spot, you could sunbathe. I found a lovely sunny area in front of one of the uglier modern houses that had been split into two flats. The front doors sat side by side; 22A and 22B, and they looked identical.

They both had 'Letting Agreed' signs standing outside, with a logo I had seen many times in this street. I enjoyed sitting in the sun for a while. There was no sign of anyone at either house yet, but I made a note to myself to come back – I knew that people would be coming soon. And after all, life was still a bit precarious. Claire loved me but wasn't at home during the day, and she was going away at the weekend. Jonathan, well, that could still go either way, despite my determination. I needed more options.

I had discovered that I could rely on myself, but that didn't suit a cat like me. I didn't want to be feral, and fighting. I wanted to be on someone's lap, or a warm blanket, being fed out of tins and given milk and affection. That was the kind of cat I was; I couldn't change that, and I really didn't want to.

The cold, lonely nights of the past few months were still fresh in my mind: the fear that had lived with me every minute; the hunger; the exhaustion. It wasn't something I would ever be able to face again, and it wasn't something I would ever forget. I needed a family, I needed love and I needed security. It was all I wanted, yearned for, and I would never ask for anything more than that.

As the sun began to disappear, I strolled back. I thought about how funny life could be. I was so lonely when Agnes died, it made me ill. I pined for her terribly and my owner took me to the dreaded vet. I had stopped eating and relieving myself, and Kathy, the vet, said that I'd given myself a bladder infection. She said it was due to grief, as she prodded and poked around. Margaret had seemed surprised; she hadn't thought that cats felt emotions like humans. Maybe it wasn't exactly the same, but it was pretty bad. I was mourning Agnes, and it had made me ill. And Claire was mourning Steve, the man in the suit, and Jonathan was mourning something called 'Singapore'. I saw the grief in them as I had felt it myself. So I decided I would be there for them, as any decent cat would be.

# Chapter
# Ten

Chapter
Ten

I called for Tiger at about lunchtime, as I wanted to show her the flats at number 22. We took a leisurely stroll up there – Tiger wasn't one for rushing around when she didn't need to – and we stopped only to tease a big ugly dog, who was shut in his front garden. The game was to go right up to the gate, and poke a paw through, making him lunge forward. Tiger and I would then jump back, which made us very happy. The dog got so angry; he was barking wildly, and flashing his snarling teeth at us. It was most fun. The dog tried to jump up, but everyone knows that cats can jump higher than dogs. I didn't think we would ever tire of this game but eventually, Tiger wanted to stop.

'I think we've embarrassed him enough,' she said. I flashed him my best cat grin as we stalked off. If he had been free he wouldn't have thought twice about chasing us and frightening us half to death. That was the way of the world.

The flats at number 22 were still empty when we got there, but as we went to the small front lawn, Tiger gave me her approval. We decided to take the back way home, so we could jump up and balance on fences, to make a change. We chased the odd bird, too, for added entertainment. It was a lovely afternoon.

I had a short cat nap and was waiting for Claire when she got home, which seemed to please her. She gave me a big, bright smile.

'Alfie, we have a guest for dinner tonight,' she said, sounding excited. She went off to shower. When she came back downstairs she was wearing a pair of jeans and a jumper, not pyjamas. She started cooking and although she poured a glass of wine as she did this, for once she wasn't crying. She fed and petted me, as she pulled things out of the fridge and put them in a pan. She was happier than I had ever seen her as she hummed to herself, and I wondered if the man in the picture was coming round. I felt afraid for her as well as optimistic.

The doorbell went and she rushed to open the door. When she did, I saw a woman who looked around the same age as Claire standing there, holding out some flowers and wine.

'Hi Tasha, come in,' Claire smiled.

'Hi Claire, what a gorgeous house,' Tasha exclaimed, cheerily, as she entered.

I watched them as Tasha took her coat off and Claire asked her if she wanted a glass of wine, before they sat down at the small dining table.

'You're my first proper visitor,' Claire said. I felt a little bit put out; I was her first proper visitor, surely?

'Well, cheers to that and welcome to London! It's good to see you out of the office.'

'Is it always that crazy at work?' Claire asked.

'Yes, or even crazier!' Tasha laughed and I immediately liked her. I settled myself under the table and brushed against her leg. She rewarded me by stroking my tail in a very lovely way – something I really enjoyed. I wanted Claire and Tasha to be friends, so I could be friends with her too.

I was right, it seemed Tasha's visit was doing her good as Claire did eat properly and I hoped that perhaps she was turning a corner. When I began to stop pining for Agnes my appetite came back, perhaps hers was too.

'So, tell me what brought you to London?' Tasha asked.

'It's a long story,' Claire replied, and she poured them both more wine before she started talking.

I stayed still under the table, huddled in the warmth of Tasha's leg, and listened as Claire filled in the blanks of her recent life. As she spoke, I could hear her voice change but I knew she wasn't crying; she went from sad, to angry, and back to sad again.

'I married Steve, after we'd been together for three years. We lived together for a year and he proposed as soon as we moved in.'

'When did you get married?' Tasha asked.

'Just over a year ago. I hadn't had much luck in love, to be honest. My mum always said I was a late starter. I didn't really have a relationship until I went to university! I was studious, I guess. But then I met Steve. I was living in Exeter, in Devon, working for a marketing consultancy, and I met him at a party. He was handsome and lovely. I fell for him straight away.'

'Right,' Tasha said, draining her glass and pouring more drinks.

'I thought he was the perfect man; funny, kind and charming. And when he proposed I thought I'd burst with happiness. I was about to turn thirty-five, I wanted children really badly, and he agreed. We said that we'd get married and enjoy a bit of a honeymoon, then try for a baby.' Claire wiped a tear from her eye. She was being stronger than I'd ever seen her, but her sadness was all around us.

'Are you sure you want to tell me?' Tasha asked, softly. Claire nodded and took a sip of her drink before continuing.

'Sorry, but I haven't spoken about it to many people.'

'Please, don't apologise.' Tasha was definitely a woman after my own heart.

'But then about three months after the wedding, he changed.

77

He became moody and short-tempered and whenever I asked what was wrong, he just snapped at me. It got to the point that I was almost too scared to speak in my own home.'

I felt many emotions listening to Claire's story; sadness, anger, and real affection for the woman who took care of me. If I ever saw this awful man, I'd scratch him across the face. And I'm not even a violent cat.

'About eight months after the wedding he told me that he'd made a terrible mistake. He had fallen in love with some-one else and he left me and moved in with her. I knew who she was, she worked in his gym. What a cliché, eh?'

'What a jerk, more like,' Tasha said.

'I know, but I feel like such a fool. I really thought that he was the one, and I had no idea that he was probably cheating on me for ages. And that's why I moved. They lived in the same area as me. Exeter is a small city and I knew that I'd probably see them all the time. I couldn't bear that.' I finally understood why Claire was here and why she cried so much. It just made me love her more – I wanted to take care of her as much as she took care of me.

'Sometimes I think that you never truly know another person,' Tasha said, sounding sad.

'Sorry,' Claire said, suddenly sitting up straight and pulling herself together, 'I haven't asked about you. You say your hus-band's called Dave?'

'Boyfriend, or "partner", if we're being PC. We've been together for ten years, neither of us wants to get married but that's more about marriage than our relationship, I hope. We're happy. We don't have children, but it's in the plans for the next year or so. Dave plays football too much and is messy and I drive him crazy in other ways, but we work.' Tasha almost looked apologetic.

'I'm glad, because then there's always hope,' Claire smiled. I realised that although I was sure she was crying because of Steve, she was also lonely in other ways and Tasha might help her with that. I knew she had me but I wasn't so vain that I didn't know she also needed human friends.

'Look, I have a book group. It's a bit lame, because we drink wine and gossip more than we talk about the books, but why don't you join us? It'd be a really good way for you to meet people and they are a really lovely bunch, even if I do say so myself.'

'I'd love to. I need to rebuild my life now, that's why I came here.'

'Let's drink to that,' she raised her glass. 'New beginnings.'

I couldn't resist it; I jumped onto the table, knowing full well that humans didn't really like that, and I raised my paw to touch the glass, which was my way of joining in. They both looked at me and laughed.

'That's an incredible cat you've got there,' Tasha said, giving me a very big fuss.

'I know, he came with the house. Although, Alfie, you shouldn't be on the table.' But Claire wasn't cross; she laughed. I grinned my cat grin and jumped down.

They both seemed happy, so I thought it might be a good time to check on my other friend, Jonathan, and see if he had received my latest present yet. They didn't seem to notice me leave via the cat flap, as they were still laughing. It seemed that Tasha made Claire happy and I was very glad of it.

It was dark and the temperature had dropped as I made my way through the back gardens to number 46. The big fat Tom who had bullied me before tried to scare me, but I just yelled as loudly as I could at him and he backed off. He was too fat to chase me anyway. I went through the cat flap and into Jonathan's immaculate kitchen. It was in darkness but I soon found him sitting on the sofa in his living room. In front of him was a computer and there was a man's face on the screen, which seemed to be talking.

'Thanks mate, I appreciate it,' Jonathan said.

'No worries.' The man on the screen spoke English but with a funny-sounding accent. He looked about the same age as Jonathan, but not so handsome.

'I'm just grateful that I've got a job, I can't cope with having nothing to do.'

'It's not quite the same as SSV, but it's a good company and it should suit you.'

'If you're ever in the UK, I'll buy you dinner,' Jonathan said.

'Same if you come to Sydney. Anyway, see you mate.'

Jonathan closed the lid on the computer and it was time for me to make my entrance. Standing as tall as I could, I lifted my tail magnificently in the air. I strode, with my best cat walk, one foot crossing over the other, and moved slowly, but purposefully, to where Jonathan was sitting.

He sighed deeply.

'You again. And I'm guessing you left me the dead bird this time?' He didn't sound as cross as he had done; I knew he would be pleased. I tilted my head and miaowed at him. I was sure he really liked the bird.

'Why do cats not understand that humans don't want dead animals in their houses?' I looked at him curiously. I understood this with some people but I knew that Jonathan was like most cats; he liked the chase and the kill, I could tell. He wouldn't admit it but I was pretty sure he was beginning to enjoy my presents. He stood up.

'Let's make a deal. If I feed you, will you leave me alone?' I tilted my head again. Once more, I knew he didn't mean it. 'It might work; after all, it seems that if I don't feed you, you come back, so maybe you're the sort of cat that prefers reverse psychology.'

I had no idea what he was talking about, but he went to the fridge, took out some prawns and dropped them in a bowl for me. He then poured me a saucer of milk.

'I'm only doing this because I'm in a good mood. I've got a job, you see,' he said, as I concentrated on the feast laid out before me; I was overjoyed. He went back to the fridge, took out a bottle, opened it and started drinking. 'I'm so relieved, I was beginning to think that I'd never get another job.' He shuddered and I kept eating.

'What on earth is wrong with me?' he asked. 'I'm talking to a bloody cat. Surely that's the second sign of madness.' I fleetingly wondered what the first sign was.

When I had finished eating, I licked my paws clean, noticing that he was watching me as he nursed a beer. When I'd finished, I went to rub his legs in thanks and then, as quickly as I had arrived, I left.

I knew how to play this man; I didn't want him to think that I was a needy cat. Alpha males didn't like needy, I had learnt that from the soap operas as well. And anyway, look how far I had come already. From being a terrified, broken-hearted, lonely little cat, to one who had survived the streets and now had two new friends to care for. I hoped Margaret and Agnes could see me from wherever they were, and that they would be proud of me.

Thinking about my old life made me sad, but despite that, I smiled to myself all the way back to Claire's. Not only had I had two dinners tonight, but now I knew for sure that Jonathan liked me and it would only be a matter of time before I could call his big house home, too.

I thought to the weekend ahead; Claire had told me she would be going to see her parents, but I knew she would leave me food. As much as I would miss her, I was quite glad she was going away, as it would give me the chance to bond properly with Jonathan. I was pretty certain that after spending more time with me he would find me irresistible. After all, it had only taken me a few days to get Agnes on side and she was far more moody and stubborn a cat than Jonathan was a man.

# Chapter
# Eleven

As Claire packed her things, I realised that she was nervous. She kept biting her lip and stopping to sit down, as if her legs didn't work properly. I prided myself on being a perceptive cat; I assumed that she was scared of bumping into that awful man, Steve, and his girlfriend. But despite this setback, Claire had been doing quite well. She and Tasha were obviously becoming friends, as Claire had decided to go along to this book club thing the following week. She was reading a book, something about a woman who planned to kill her husband. Claire said it would probably have given her ideas had she still been married; it was cheaper than a divorce, apparently. I hoped she would make more friends at the book club. I wanted Claire to be happy again more than anything. I almost felt that my happiness was irrevocably tied up with hers, now.

After a couple of weeks with Claire, I already loved her. I knew because of the way I had loved Agnes and Margaret. Margaret was a beautiful person. She was always smiling, even when she was struggling, and she wanted to help others although she could have done with a lot of help herself. She was a huge inspiration to me and she made me the cat I was.

Claire needed my love and it was my duty to give it. I stayed close to Claire as she packed, giving her extra rubs and making sure she knew I was there. As she took her bag downstairs, she turned to me and picked me up.

'Are you sure you're going to be OK when I'm away?' she asked, her eyes full of concern.

I tipped my head as if to say 'Of course.'

'There's plenty of food; just take care. I'll miss you.' She kissed me on the tip of my nose, something she'd never done before. I purred in thanks.

A car honked its horn and she gave me a last stroke before she left the house, locking the door behind her. I hoped that she would be all right and the horrible Steve wouldn't upset her this weekend, and then I went out.

I greeted a couple of younger cats that were playing in the street and carried on walking to the end of the road to have another look at the house split into two. I wondered if anyone had moved in to the flats yet. I stopped short when I saw a man and a woman by the closed front door of 22A. The woman had something tied to her chest which, on closer inspection, seemed to be a noisily crying baby. The man had his arm around her. She was very beautiful; tall with long blonde hair and green eyes that any cat would be envious of, to be frank. I stayed back so I could observe them for a bit as they locked the door of their new home. Inside, I was jumping for joy; there were three of them, and despite the fact that one of them was smaller than me, it meant a household with three more people to take care of me, rather than one.

I edged closer so I could hear what they were saying.

'Don't worry, Pol, it's going to be lovely when we get the furniture in.' The man was taller than the woman, and he was kind looking, although lacking in hair.

'I don't know, Matt, it's such a long way from Manchester, and so much smaller than our old house.'

'Think of it as just a temporary step, it's a rental and as soon as we're settled, we'll get somewhere better. Darling, you do know that I couldn't turn this job down, it's for our future; ours and little Henry's.' He leant over and kissed the top of the head, which had stopped crying.

'I know, but I'm scared. I'm terrified.' She looked as frightened as I had felt when I first started my journey to Edgar Road.

'Honestly, we'll be fine, Polly. We can move in tomorrow when the furniture arrives, out of the cramped hotel room into our first home in London, so that's something positive. This is a new start for us; for us as a family.'

I immediately liked Matt as he took Polly into his arms and enveloped his wife and child the way a proper man should. Yes, I instinctively knew that this would be a good household for me to be part of. They walked away together, and I decided that I would visit them again once they'd moved in. That would be a better time to introduce myself.

I had a spring in my step as I jumped through Jonathan's cat flap. You see, I knew he liked me, as he hadn't followed through with his threat to get rid of it. I found him sitting in the living room on the computer again. I managed to look at the screen; there wasn't a person there, but photographs of shiny cars. I jumped up next to him.

'Oh, it's you again? I guess you didn't understand my deal last night.' I wanted to tell him that I understood it but I just didn't agree with it, so I miaowed loudly, hoping that would do.

'I guess I should at least be thankful that you haven't brought me anything dead today.' My heart dropped; I felt terrible to be turning up empty handed. I lay down and put my head on the keyboard. I thought he might be cross, but luckily he laughed.

'Come on, you can have the rest of the prawns. They'd only be thrown away.' I licked my lips and followed him to the kitchen. He tipped the prawns into a bowl and I ate them greedily. I wasn't hungry, but fresh prawns were a huge treat. When I finished eating, I noticed he was dressed nicely tonight; not a suit, but not scruffy. I looked at him with my eyes slightly closed, suspiciously.

'Right, Alfie the Unwanted, I'm going out on the town tonight. If I were you, I wouldn't wait up.' He laughed and, before I knew it, he'd slunk out the front door.

I had two homes but I was still alone. In my old house, I had rarely been on my own. If Margaret went out, then Agnes would be there, and after Agnes died, Margaret would only leave the house for such a short time that I barely even noticed that she was gone.

I couldn't wait for the new family at 22A to move in. This cat had needs; food, water, warm shelter, laps and love. That was all I required but after what I had been through in my short life, I wasn't taking any chances. I decided to go to sleep on Jonathan's expensive looking sofa for now, and despite what he had said, I would wait up for him, because without Claire here he was the only family I had.

# Chapter
# Twelve

I was daydreaming about the past. About living in my old house with Margaret and Agnes. The day was cold, and Agnes was in a lot of pain. Margaret had phoned the vet, who had said the end was imminent. If Margaret wanted to take her in she would give Agnes something to help the pain; it was either that, or put her to sleep.

Margaret sobbed, a bit like Claire had been doing, tears filled with grief ran down her sunken cheeks. I wanted to join in, but Agnes was trying so hard to be brave that I suppressed my own emotion and I snuggled into her, hoping that I wasn't adding to her pain. Margaret was getting ready to take her to the vet, which wasn't very easy as Margaret was old and didn't have a car – she could barely lift the cat carrier any more. She phoned her neighbour, a nice man called Don, who wasn't much younger than Margaret and he said that he would take her. He was always happy to help Margaret. Agnes said that she thought at one stage they might end up together, after Don's wife died a few years back, but Margaret was far too fond of her own company, as she was often heard to say.

'All I need is myself and my cats,' she used to say, laughing. I could almost hear her voice now.

Back then, I had to stay at home while they took Agnes to the vet. Left in the house alone, I yowled louder than I ever had before. I was so scared about losing Agnes. Even if she came home, I knew there wasn't much longer in her, I'd heard Margaret talking about that.

Agnes did come home, and I was so excited. I was so

thankful, I licked her. I had thought I would never see her face again, and although she was quiet, she was there, by my side, where she should have been. I was euphoric. But by the morning she was gone. I knew because I slept with her and at some point when I woke I noticed her heart had stopped beating. I had gone from feeling so happy to completely wretched in the space of a few hours.

At that point in time, it was the worst day of my life.

My sad thoughts were interrupted by a key in the door, followed by howls of laughter and a clacking of heels. The house remained in darkness as I heard footsteps enter the room and then, just as I was about to stretch, someone fell on me.

I yelped as loudly as I could. A woman's voice screamed. Jonathan put on the light and looked a bit cross.

'What are you doing on my sofa?' he asked, sounding angry. I would have liked to have asked him the same thing; after all, I was there first. Instead I jumped off and stood in the room surveying the situation.

The woman wasn't the woman from before. She was tall and thin and had a very short skirt which showed off very long legs.

'Is that your cat?' the woman asked, slurring her words slightly. What was it with humans getting drunk?

'No, it's my bloody squatter,' Jonathan replied glaring at me. I didn't know what a squatter was, but it didn't sound good. The woman approached him again and flung her arms around him. As they started kissing, I decided that it was time for me to leave. After all, I had often heard it said that three was a crowd.

It was light outside as I awoke on Claire's bed. Skipping downstairs, I stopped to eat one of the bowls of food that Claire had left for me and drink some water, before taking an early morning walk. It wasn't exactly Jonathan's prawns, but at least I was well fed. I decided to give him a wide berth until later, when perhaps his guest had left. So instead I went to check on the progress of the number 22 flats.

Although it was early, the tall woman and the baby were there in the front garden and the man was unloading furniture from a white van. The woman, despite her beauty, looked very worried. She was constantly biting her lip and sighing. Yet again, it seemed I was drawn to a human in need. Although I didn't know what her need was yet.

'I've got to go and feed Henry,' she said, as the sound of a baby's wail started up from inside.

'OK, Polly, I'll carry on here.'

I followed the woman inside; it was a house without stairs, all on one level. It was a fairly small space that looked as if it was almost ready to be lived in. There was a serious amount of unpacking to do, but there was a large grey sofa and a matching chair, which Polly went to sit on, with her baby. She stuck him to her chest and he stopped crying immediately. I was incredibly curious; I'd seen this on television but not in real life. It brought back very vague and unreliable memories of how my mother used to nurse me before we were weaned and I went to live with Margaret. It made me feel even more nostalgic about my past. Suddenly the woman looked at me. I blinked in greeting but as I prepared to introduce myself, she screamed loudly. The baby started crying and the man ran into the room.

'What's wrong?' he asked, his voice full of concern.

'There's a cat here!' she shrieked, as she tried to resettle the baby back on her. I was a little offended; I hadn't had quite that reaction before. Not even from Jonathan.

'Polly, it's a cat, I'm not sure you need to be quite so upset.' Matt spoke gently, as if he was speaking to a child. Her baby was quiet again but now it was Polly's turn to start crying. I realised I might have made a huge mistake; this woman clearly had an extreme phobia of cats. I wasn't sure that such a thing existed but she certainly seemed scared of me.

'But I've read that cats kill babies.' I yelped as if I'd been hit. I'd been accused of many things in my life; killing birds and mice and even, if needs must, the occasional rabbit, but I'd never killed a baby. Perish the thought.

'Pol,' the man went and knelt down next to her. 'Cats don't kill babies. They just say to make sure they are not in the room when the baby is in their cot, in case they go and sleep on them and accidentally smother them. This cat is awake, and you've got Henry.' I liked him even more than I had at first; his voice was gentle and full of patience.

'Are you sure?' She seemed more than a little neurotic to me. I could tell that there was something wrong with this woman. Not in the way there was with Claire, but there was definitely something that wasn't right.

'How on earth can the cat kill Henry while you're here?' He came over and picked me up. He was a nice man, I decided; he held me firmly but gently. You can tell a lot from a man from the way they hold you. Jonathan was a little too rough, but this man was just right.

'Matt, I just . . .' Polly looked upset still.

'His name is Alfie,' he said, reading my tag. 'Hello, Alfie,' he added, giving me a stroke. He had nice hands and I rubbed my head against him. 'Anyway, he doesn't live here, Polly, so you've got nothing to worry about. He must have just crept in while the front door was open. Where do you live?' he asked me, and I gave him my most charming miaow.

'How can you be sure that he doesn't live here?'

'He's got a name tag. There's a number on it. I'll call it if it'll make you feel better.'

'No, no, I'm sure you're right. Just make sure you put him out.'

Polly still looked unsure. The baby seemed to be asleep on her and I felt that although this man was nice, there was definitely sadness in the small, square room.

'Right, well, I'll go and finish unloading. Come on Alfie, time for you to go home.' He carried me outside and gently put me on the doorstep. I hadn't had a chance to look round the rest of the flat, but I didn't want to risk upsetting Polly again.

I had a few hours to fill before dinner time so I thought that perhaps it was time to find Jonathan another present. After all, now I was winning him over, I needed to step up my charm offensive. It would be useful to have him onside because I definitely had my work cut out with Polly.

# Chapter
# Thirteen

Chapter
Thirteen

I left number 22A, having made the decision to get a present for Jonathan, but was distracted by the bright sunlight. I had been told many times that cats should hunt at night; that this was meant to be our favourite nocturnal activity, but I'd never been much of a going-out-at-night cat and nowadays, I only went out at night if I absolutely had to, after my terrifying journey.

There were plenty of birds flying overhead but as I sat on a grassy verge by the local park, I saw some butterflies fluttering around. I made a few unsuccessful attempts to leap at them, but they managed to get away. Then I spotted some resting on a nearby bush. Unable to resist, I started chasing them. It had been one of my favourite games back when I lived with Margaret. I pounced this way and that, and the butterfly escaped my paws every time. Getting slightly out of breath, I made one last attempt and leapt for it into a large leafed bush, but I misread the distance and instead fell and landed on my bottom. A passing bird laughed at me. Although I was bruised, and a little embarrassed, it had been fun. I mustered my dignity, hauled myself up and decided to abandon hunting or chasing for another day.

I found a sunny spot to rest, where I accidentally fell asleep. I must have slept for a long time, because when I was awoken by two of the neighbourhood cats having a screeching row over who was the best looking, it was getting dark. The argument wasn't that unusual, cats can be vain. They asked me to choose, but I knew the dangers of getting involved, so I told them they were both fine looking cats and diplomatically slid off.

With Claire still away, I went back to Jonathan's. I let myself in through the cat flap, finding the house in darkness. I padded through the empty kitchen and into the living room. I was surprised to find Jonathan lying on the sofa. He was resting his head on a cushion as if he was asleep, but his eyes were open. There was no sign of the woman from last night; he was alone, once again. He looked at me as I walked in, and I felt bad that I'd come empty handed. He looked as if he really needed a present.

'You're back,' he said, dryly. 'I'd almost say I'm pleased to see you. At least the house isn't so damn empty any more.' I miaowed a 'thank you' although I wasn't sure how much of a compliment it was. Despite that, I decided to chance my luck and I jumped up on the sofa and sat next to him. He looked at me but he didn't tell me to get off, which was progress of sorts.

'Where do you go when you're not here?' he asked, suddenly. I miaowed. 'Do you just roam the streets? Because I get the feeling that you actually live with me.' He looked confused and I purred my assent. 'It's funny, Alfie, but it's hit me that this is my life now. I live in this empty house which is too big for me, and I have barely any friends.' I wondered about the two women I'd met here so far. 'And we can't count my one night stands. I don't know how I got to the age of forty-three, with nothing meaningful to show for my life,' he continued, sounding self-pitying. 'No wife, no family, and only a handful of friends, most of whom are in different countries.' I moved closer to him and tried to purr compassionately.

'It's just me and you, Alfie. All I have for my forty-three years is a bloody cat to talk to, and I don't even know if you're mine.'

I looked at him, head tilted to one side, trying to be reassuring.

'I guess you're hungry?' he said, and I miaowed as loudly as I could. This was more like it. I was famished. I followed him into the kitchen where he took some smoked salmon out of the fridge. As much as I loved Claire, dinner with Jonathan was really special. He put some on a plate on the floor for me and he stroked me as I started eating, in a tender way that he'd never done before. We were indulging in some male bonding.

Although I was surprised, I concentrated on eating. I could be a bit of an emotional cat and I definitely felt my heart warming; I was touched. I had been determined that I would crack Jonathan, otherwise I wouldn't have kept coming back, but I hadn't imagined I would do so quite as quickly as this. If I hadn't been so busy eating, I would have been jumping for joy.

After we had both had dinner, we went back to the living room. We were a bit of an odd couple; a big man and a little cat. My heart swelled with happiness as we sat on the sofa together. Jonathan turned on a huge TV and started watching something which involved a lot of violence and men with guns. I could hardly believe I was allowed to sit with him, snuggled up on the sofa. Distractedly, he stroked me as he watched his programme, and although I didn't like what was on the TV, I really liked the comfort he was giving me so I didn't move an inch. It strengthened my resolve to make sure I gave Jonathan the help that I knew in my heart he needed.

# Chapter
# Fourteen

I woke very early; I knew because it was still dark. I was a little surprised to see that I was still on Jonathan's sofa. He hadn't kicked me off, but left me sleeping. I must have fallen asleep whilst he was watching that gruesome film. I was reluctant to leave, but I really wanted to go to Claire's, eat some breakfast, and then go and wait at 22A for any movement. I wondered if 22B would be occupied soon, and what the new family there would be like. Perhaps I would visit only the nicest of the two; I still hadn't forgiven Polly for calling me a baby killer.

When I arrived, after my morning meal, there was a van outside the building and the door to the other flat was open. It wasn't a smart looking vehicle, like the one that Matt and Polly had had their furniture delivered in the previous day but a slightly battered, dark blue van that looked as if it might have hit a lot of lamp posts and run over a lot of animals. I shuddered – hopefully not cats. Two men were unloading furniture from it, which they were carrying into the house. I peered into the open front door. 22B was an upstairs flat. As soon as you opened the door there was a small space and then stairs. I was tempted to go in, but I held back as the men carried a table into the flat. They were struggling to negotiate the small space with the piece of furniture, and I sensed the danger of getting involved. They were speaking in a language I didn't recognise. Their voices were quite loud and animated as if they were rowing, although I didn't think they were. Mind you, seeing them have to carry the furniture up the steep flight of stairs, if they had been, I guess you couldn't blame them. I hung back for a while, still itching to go inside, but fearful and unsure. Not only because the men were quite big, but also because of the language I didn't understand. What if they were from a place where they ate cats? I didn't know if such a place existed but I didn't want to take any chances. Agnes had told me tales of countries where they ate dogs. Apparently it was normal for some cultures. I shuddered again. I didn't want to end my life in anyone's cooking pot.

I wanted to find out more about the people who lived here, though. I lay low in the shadows as I saw the men come back downstairs. Despite the fact that I thought I was being discreet, one of the men spotted me and came over to pet me. I blinked a 'hello' and he looked as if he blinked back. Although he seemed huge, he was surprisingly gentle with me and I purred at him. He seemed to blink quite a lot as he spoke to me in his strange language, and then a woman appeared and joined him. She was quite small but very pretty, with dark hair and brown eyes. She crouched down to pet me.

'He don't speak Polish,' the man said, giving her a kiss.

'Cats no speaking, Thomasz, she replied, in an accented voice. They both laughed and then went back to communicating in their original language. They looked to be about the same age as Polly and Matt, I guessed, and they seemed very kind and friendly. The woman's smile was really infectious and made me want to smile, although of course I did so with my eyes, by squinting at her. I'm not sure she noticed though, she was busy talking to both the men and I still couldn't understand a word they were saying.

'He still here,' she said, suddenly turning her attention back to me.

'Maybe he welcome us here,' the man joked.

'Maybe. Nice cat I think.' Her smile disappeared suddenly and she turned to the man, clinging to him and looking scared. I tilted my head to one side, intrigued, as she said something in the funny language again.

'Franceska, it will be OK. We come here for a better life. For us and the boys. I promise you it will be good.' He took her in his big arms and although she was crying, she managed to smile too. Another friend in need for me, it seemed. I had a radar, and I felt that this street had given me a purpose in life; helping people.

Relieved that I felt needed, I smiled to myself; I was learning that humans were more complicated than I thought. But they were friendly, and although the woman was sad, I saw a strength in her that neither Claire nor Polly seemed to have. I was sure that I would be welcome here, and I looked forward to coming back. I watched the woman go inside, before realising that it was sunny and bright and therefore time for me to go and get my second meal of the day.

Stalking through the cat flap, I found Jonathan sitting at the kitchen table, eating toast and drinking coffee, dressed in sportswear. I miaowed loudly, to announce that I was there.

'Hello, you. I'm guessing you want to eat?' I jumped up on the chair next to him, and he laughed.

'OK mate, hang on a minute. Let me finish my toast.' I sat and waited, patiently. I think Jonathan had made a massive mistake somewhere along the line. I don't mean the work thing he told me about, but the house. It was so empty with just him there, almost mocking him; taunting him that he was alone. If I was him, I would have chosen something smaller that didn't seem so empty with just him and me to fill it. One of the flats at number 22 would probably have suited him better. I understood now why he spoke to me; like Claire, it was loneliness. I began to realise that I wasn't the only one to have suffered from feeling excessive loneliness; I saw it in Claire, I saw it here, and I'd seen something like it, although perhaps not quite the same, in Polly and Franceska.

There was much for a small cat like me to ponder; there was even more for me to do to put things right.

Jonathan fed me some tuna from a tin, which wasn't quite as good as the fresh prawns or smoked salmon, but I wasn't one to complain.

'I'm going to the gym, Alfie. Need to make sure I don't get fat living here on my own like a mad man with only a cat to talk to.' I was startled at his revelation but then he laughed, and I felt relieved. Of course he wasn't mad, he was just a little unhinged.

I decided to go and get some exercise as well. I'd eaten twice already and the fact that I was now being fed in two homes was something I had to consider. Of course, I didn't want to give up eating the food; the memory of struggling to eat for days meant that I would never snub another meal in my life. But if the people at number 22 started feeding me as well, then it wouldn't be just Jonathan getting fat, but me too. And there was no way that that could happen. I'd never fit in the cat flaps for a start.

Despite the fact I was visiting different houses in the street, which meant I stalked between them, I was aware I had become a bit lazy, the way I was in my old life with Margaret. I was also looking better, being a much heartier weight. However, I still couldn't chance being too lazy or complacent. What if I had to somehow survive on my own again? And although I shuddered at the thought, I knew it was a possibility. Hopefully not one I'd face, but one I had to be prepared for, this time, as I was never going to take chances ever again.

# Chapter
# Fifteen

I was curled up in the special cat bed Claire had bought me, when I heard her key in the lock. My new bed was blue and white striped, and although it was not as comfortable as my old cat basket, it was pretty nice. Claire made a bee-line straight for me and gave me a huge fuss, which I really appreciated. I was also relieved. I had been worried she might come back crying; I had even fretted that she might not come back at all. 'I've missed you Alfie,' she said, and I felt my heart warming, 'I hope you missed me.' She was smiling and she looked better. She was still too thin, of course, reminding me of how I was when she first met me. But her hair was glossy and her cheeks had some colour in them. It looked as if the weekend away had done her good.

For a moment, I panicked that it might mean that she would move back there, where she came from, but then I tried to calm myself. She was here, wasn't she? She had come back; I had to focus on that. I knew I worried far too much for a cat, but that was the consequence of my past. I was learning that I was drawn to helping people who mirrored the feelings I had experienced. The attraction seemed so strong that I knew it was important for me to do whatever I could for them.

She went to the kitchen to feed me and she put the kettle on and made a cup of tea.

After I'd eaten, she went to get a bag and came back with various toys for me. There was a thing that slightly resembled a mouse on a bit of string, a ball, some more catnip, and something that jangled. I rubbed up against her legs, in thanks; but in reality, I would have been just as happy with a shoelace. I'd never been much of a toy cat, not even as a kitten, but that was mainly because Agnes was so disdainful of that sort of thing. I wanted to impress her, so I too would act as if the toys were beneath me. I made an effort to play with them to please Claire, though. I wouldn't want her to think me ungrateful.

I chased the ball under the sofa, and then almost got stuck trying to retrieve it. I batted it with my paw and it rolled back out. As I emerged, I saw Claire laughing. She clapped her hands in delight. So then I tried to pick up the jangly thing with my paws but it slipped out and across the floor. I chased it again; it made a very strange tinkling noise. Every time I thought I'd got the toy, it slipped from my grasp, so I ended up going backwards and forwards across the room, which was infuriating. Claire seemed to find this delightful, although I couldn't for the life of me understand why.

She went upstairs, saying something about unpacking, and I decided to have another rest; playing was hard work. Also, the meal I had just wolfed down had made me sleepy – it was time for a cat nap. I awoke to laughter; a fairly alien sound in Claire's household, so I was immediately alert. Tasha appeared and picked me up, making a huge fuss of me as she nestled into my neck.

'Hello, gorgeous,' she said. She was definitely a cat person and I wondered why she didn't have her own cat as she seemed to like me so much. I knew she didn't, as I would have detected the smell on her.

Claire reappeared, carrying two glasses.

'He'll want to live with you, if you carry on like that,' she said, laughing. Oh, where had the miserable Claire gone? She seemed like a different person. I couldn't wait to hear what had caused this change.

'I wish I could take him home, but unfortunately my other half is allergic to cats, so I just have to enjoy him here.'

'Oh how awful, really allergic?'

'Yes, I need to shower when I get home from here and wash my clothes, that's how bad he is. Of course, if he's been an idiot, I might just forget . . . ' They both laughed. I felt a bit affronted. I wasn't sure that being allergic to me should be a laughing matter. What kind of person was allergic to cats?

Claire left the room again and reappeared with some plates of food. She put them on the dining table, and they both sat down. To my amazement and delight, Claire ate. She ate more than I had ever seen her eat. I wanted to jump for joy, my Claire was definitely getting better, but I decided not to startle her by making a fuss.

'So, do tell,' Tasha said. 'Something good obviously happened this weekend.'

'Oh God, I feel so much better. Like I've completed the first quest in a mission, or something. I confronted my demons and survived them! You know, going home and risking bumping into them. And I did!' Claire sounded almost gleeful and I tried to understand, but at the moment, it was beyond my limited comprehension.

'Where?' Tasha asked, her eyes wide.

'Mum and I went to the supermarket. She still treats me like I'm five and she insisted on stocking up on food for me to bring home. Honestly, she acts like there are no supermarkets in London.'

'Claire, get to the point,' Tasha pushed, with a giggle.

'Sorry, anyway, so we're in the vegetable aisle and suddenly they both appear. Him pushing a trolley, and her moaning about something. I saw them before they saw me and neither of them looked happy.' Claire, however, looked very happy.

'What was she saying?' Tasha and I were riveted.

'No idea, but anyway, she was fat. I mean fatter than she ever was before they got together, and first I worried she was pregnant,' Claire said.

'Was she?'

'No, but I'll get to that. Mum was grabbing my arm for dear life, and then we came face to face. He didn't look great, if I'm honest. But maybe that was because I was seeing him properly for the first time.'

'Without your rose-tinted glasses?'

'Exactly. Anyway, he said "hello" and I said "hello". She stood with her mouth wide open, and I was relieved I'd put on nice clothes and done my hair and make-up.'

'I told you to look your best at all times, just in case you saw the bastard.'

'Yes, thank goodness I listened to you!' She laughed and I wanted to give her a kiss, which I did, but on her arm, as she was still talking. I was proud of my Claire, although I wasn't sure exactly why. 'So, then I asked how they were, and they mumbled that they were fine, but I'm not sure they were. I mean I know I'm too thin, I do see that now, but how on earth can she have put on about three stone in a couple of months? She looked nothing like the woman he left me for. Anyway the worst bit is that, while I was civil, my mother stood beside me, quiet as a mouse, and then suddenly, from nowhere, she asked when the baby was due!'

'Nooo, she didn't?'

'She did. I should have felt a bit smug, as she stormed off and Steve mumbled that there wasn't a baby, but I almost felt sorry for them. I don't know why. I mean, she knew he was married when she slept with him, and they nearly destroyed me with their behaviour, but I actually felt sorry for them. Which is brilliant!' Claire and Tasha hugged, and giggled like school children.

I miaowed my approval. I might not know much but I've seen on the TV how relationships can ruin humans' lives, to the point where I wonder if it wouldn't be a better world if people were like cats? Of course we know love, but when it comes to romance, we are too wise to the way of the cat world to put all our kittens in one basket; we are necessarily pragmatic. I do find some female cats attractive, actually most of them, but I am not naive enough to think that we will be monogamous for life. Cats may be together for only a few days, or weeks, or months if we're lucky, but then we either have kittens or we move on. Perhaps if humans fixated less on having to be with one person for the rest of their lives, they might actually find that life works a bit better for them?

'So going home was a good thing after all, despite your reluctance?'

'Not only because I saw them, and actually it didn't upset me the way I was sure it would, but it made me feel that moving here wasn't just running away any more. I want to be in London; with a good job and prospects, my lovely little home, Alfie, and of course my new friends. I actually enjoyed being home but I wanted to come back. I'm not completely fine, I know that, but I'll admit some of the fear has gone.'

'Well, this calls for a celebration. End of this week, I'll organise a girls' night out. We'll hit the town and go to some of the best bars in London. Plenty of cocktails and cute men.'

'You know what, I think I'm ready.'

'Had she really put on three stone?' Tasha asked.

'I don't know exactly, but she had definitely put on *a lot*. And unlike me, she didn't really need to.'

I was now under the table, and I snuggled into Claire's legs, trying to convey to her that I was proud of her transformation. It was similar, of course, to my own, but now she needed to eat properly and drink less wine, and well, she might be as good as me. It seemed clear that Claire was now ready for her new beginning.

'To new beginnings,' she said, as she raised her glass. I wondered if she could read my mind as I jumped on the table and tried to join in with the toast.

By the time that Claire and Tasha had nearly finished a second bottle, and were talking nonsense, I decided to sneak out to check on Jonathan. Now Claire was happier, I thought it might be time to concentrate a bit more on finding Jonathan's smile. I had recognised a need in Claire that I knew, because I had been in her position, in my own way, and I felt as if I had been able to comfort and calm her. Now I had to do the same with Jonathan. We had made progress but there was still a way to go. I had my work cut out for me; that was for sure.

I entered through the cat flap and found him in the living room, lying on the sofa again. He looked at me but didn't even say anything, which wasn't like him. There was no insult or greeting; he almost looked through me. He went back to staring at the TV, but he looked bad. His hair was a mess and he was wearing his pyjamas. He looked as if he had been there for a long time.

I didn't know what to do, but I went and sat next to him and miaowed gently.

'If you're hungry, you're out of luck. I'm not moving,' he

said, sounding cross. Then he leant over and he stroked me as if to say he wasn't cross. Mixed messages again. I wanted to tell him that I had just had a lovely meal and I had only come to be kind, but I wasn't sure that my miaows conveyed that, exactly. I gave it a try. Jonathan wasn't the sort of human that I found easy to figure out, but then perhaps I wasn't an easy cat to figure out either. All I knew was that underneath his tough exterior, he was lonely and scared. I saw the fear in him as I had felt it in myself.

I cocked my head to one side and tried again to tell him I wasn't hungry – I was just worried about him. I snuggled into him, rubbing my head against him, trying to convey that I was there for him, and when I saw him looking at me with tears brimming in his eyes, I was pretty sure he understood.

'Why do I feel like you're looking into my bloody soul?' he said, sounding irritated again. I didn't know how to respond. 'Well, if you do, you'll see a black hole. Or maybe nothing at all. There's nothing there. Anyway, I've got to work tomorrow; my shitty new job.' He sighed. 'But at least it's a job. Better than withering away here. Anyway, come on, if you're staying, you can come up to bed with me.' To my total surprise he picked me up and carried me upstairs, plonking me down on a chair in his bedroom which was covered with the softest blanket I had ever felt.

'I must be mad, that's my best cashmere blanket,' he sighed, as he put me down. He got into bed and almost immediately started snoring really loudly.

# Chapter
# Sixteen

The following morning was busy and a little exhausting. I woke up at Jonathan's; it was dark as he rushed around getting ready for his new job. He was muttering as he went to shower. Still wet and glistening but with a towel tied around him, he made a coffee. He didn't eat anything, but quickly laid down a saucer of milk for me. He rushed back upstairs and came down looking very smart, but mumbling under his breath as he struggled to tie his tie. I left the house with him, trying to show my support as I followed him down the street. He was swearing and huffing and puffing which I knew was his way of masking his nerves.

'Right, Alfie,' he said. 'I best go and face the first day back in the real world. Wish me luck.' I rubbed up against his legs in order to do so. 'Great, you'd better not have covered me in your bloody hair,' he muttered, but then he leant down and patted my head before running off down the street. It was obvious that Jonathan loved me, but he certainly didn't like to show his softer side.

I followed him and tried very hard to keep up with my little legs; I wanted him to see the support I was giving him. He shook his head and laughed as he increased his pace. Breathlessly, we made it to the end of the street and as he went to cross the road, I knew I had to leave him there. I didn't want to risk going further from Edgar Road than I felt comfortable with.

Still a bit fatigued from my run, I rushed back to Claire's, where she had just emerged from the shower.

'Ah, there you are,' she picked me up and kissed me. 'Where

on earth have you been? I was worried.' I snuggled into her, to try to ensure she wasn't upset with me. 'Maybe you do the cat thing of prowling through the night?' She did look a bit confused as she said this, but luckily she didn't seem cross. 'But if you do, make sure you're careful,' she finished.

She put me down and I sat on the chair next to her bed as she got ready. Humans were funny, using a contraption to wash – we have our own inbuilt shower – and then wrapping themselves in towels and clothes. Being a cat was so much easier. We kept our fur on all the time, cleaning ourselves wherever we wanted. In actual fact, we washed ourselves and combed our fur simultaneously; cats were much better designed than humans. And we certainly didn't need to go to work – something they all seemed to spend a lot of time obsessing over. Although, I was finding that keeping my new families happy was quite hard work, so perhaps I did understand that a bit more now. Claire needed sympathy, Jonathan needed my patience, they both needed my love and help, and at the same time I was also beginning to court the attention of the families in the flats at number 22. Speaking of which, it was time for me to find out what was happening down there.

Lack of exercise was no longer a problem for me as I bounded down the street towards 22A and 22B, feeling in a good cat mood. It was another sunny morning and I could almost smell the warmth as it began to permeate the air. It would be a hot day, I could tell, and for me, with my lovely fur coat, that would mean finding a spot that was sunny but not too hot and not too cool. I liked the sun, but no cat liked getting overheated. Sleeping in a nicely shaded spot was one of my favourite things in the world.

I was very excited to see the door to number 22B open,

and two children playing on the small lawn at the front of the building. Although it was shared with 22A, there was no sign of Polly or her crying baby, although I swear I could hear him, as I joined the two boys on the lawn. That wailing sound he made was almost louder than any crying I could do, even in my most heartbroken moments.

The two boys were different sizes, but they were both quite small, and I could hear one of them chatting away to himself, using words I couldn't quite make out. Suddenly, he spotted me and came up.

'Cat,' he said, very clearly, and laughed. I went to make friends with him, rubbing my head on his legs, which made him giggle. The younger boy, who had sat down to play with a toy car, laughed too. The woman I'd met before, Franceska, appeared at the door.

'Hello, Alfie cat,' she said. The boy said something to her. 'Speaking English, Aleksy,' she said gently, and yet again I wondered where they were from.

'Mamma, is cat,' he repeated, and she went up to him and gave him a kiss.

'You are clever boy,' she said, before she scooped up the smaller child. 'We give him food?'

'Yes, Mamma.' Aleksy ran ahead into the house and Franceska hung back.

'Come, Alfie,' she commanded, and I felt touched at both the invitation and that she had remembered my name. Her accent was quite hard-sounding but I liked her. She had a lovely, gentle way about her; a quality that Jonathan certainly didn't possess.

We climbed the stairs to their flat, Franceska carrying the smaller boy, and I wondered at how strange it was to cut a house in two. It was something that I found quite puzzling. The flat itself was nice enough, it was bright and modern, but it was also square and small. The stairs led to a small hallway and as I explored, I walked into the living room where there were two small, soft looking sofas which took up most of the space; a spattering of toys and a wooden coffee table. At the end of the room was a dining table and past that, an opening which led to a small kitchen. Unlike Claire's house, there were things scattered which made it a bit messy and lived-in. And unlike Jonathan's, it was very short on space.

I thought about how strange humans were. Jonathan had this big house just for him and yet here were four people (despite the fact two of them were quite small), in a space that was so compact. I didn't understand how that worked, but it didn't seem very fair. While Franceska busied herself with the boys, I went to snoop. There was a small corridor leading away from the stairs and I found two bedrooms, one which had a cot and a bed in it, the other a double bed. Outside the bedroom was a small, very white bathroom. The bedroom with the cot and bed was quite messy; there were toys scattered all over the floor. The other bedroom was neater and quite plain. There was nothing wrong with the place but I worried that it was too small for a growing family.

After I finished snooping, I joined them. The boys were sat on one of the sofas, side by side. The younger one was clutching a soggy biscuit. Aleksy was pleased to see me and started stroking me, and tickling my neck. It felt nice. Many of my cat friends and acquaintances sang the praises of children, and with Aleksy's little hands, and his warm smile, I was beginning to understand why.

Franceska returned to the room.

'We can give him fish, when we have the lunch,' she said. My ears pricked up excitedly. 'And then maybe you can practise your English on him. Me too,' she laughed. 'And I should phone the number on the tag to make sure he's not lost.' I narrowed my eyes. Claire and Jonathan hadn't changed my tag, so luckily the number was Margaret's old one. My plan was safe for now.

'Can he live here?' Aleksy asked.

'No, *kochanie*. We live in flat. We no allowed pets.' Goodness, I was taken aback. Imagine, being banned from anywhere! That was so unfair.

'It is not easy,' he said to me, sadly, as she returned to the kitchen. 'I speaking Polish in my old house. I learn English before I come here, but hard.' I snuggled into him, as he looked like he might cry, and he cuddled me, holding on so tightly that I struggled to breathe. I let him squeeze me, though, for as long as I could bear it before I had to wriggle out of his clutches. Yet again, I had found people who needed me. They were far away from home, maybe even further than I had come, and they possessed a sadness that I seemed to have a cat's sense for these days.

Bringing me back to the present, the smaller child started pawing at me then, with his grubby hands, and although I didn't mind, I made a note that I would need a good wash when I finally got out of there.

I hadn't had much contact with small children. When I lived with Margaret, there was a young girl who visited from time to time and she was fun, always wanting to play with me and feed me food from her plate, but that was my only experience. Then when I started my nomadic existence and I met other cats, one of the suggestions was that I should find a family with children.

They suggested that it was the most fun, like having friends – but friends who fed you and loved you and looked after you and played with you. In this flat, I felt I was getting that.

Although I was fond of Claire and Jonathan, I couldn't pretend that they gave me all I wanted. Yes I was fed and fussed sometimes, but I was also left on my own. It had vaguely occurred to me at this point that it might seem my doorstep antics could lead me into a bit of a pickle, but you see, I did, to a point, have a plan.

I couldn't rely just on Claire. I didn't know that she was on her own when I had chosen her house – I had been expecting at least two people. And when I went into Jonathan's house, I had been expecting a family, not a grumpy single man, so that didn't turn out as I'd planned either. I was worried that my home life was still too precarious and that had led me here. It all made perfect sense in my head. It was like the number 22 flats could be my daytime homes, and the other houses my evening abodes. I was sure I could make it work and I was determined to do so.

So I rolled onto my back to let Aleksy tickle my tummy, and I flipped my tail up in delight when I was on all fours again. Afterwards, Aleksy wanted me to hide under the chair and jump out at him. I wasn't sure why this made him and Thomasz so happy, but I was pleased to do it. I then pretended I was chasing an invisible bird which seemed to make both boys shriek with laughter.

After playing for a bit, Franceska returned and picked up the younger boy.

'The phone number no work. Maybe they change it without changing the tag.' She looked thoughtful. 'Thomasz, sleeping time.' She took him down the corridor, and returned a little later without him. I heard him crying a bit, before going quiet. Aleksy was drawing something at the coffee table and I sat on the sofa, not sure of my next move but feeling quite comfortable.

'So, Aleksy, Thomasz sleeping, we do our English,' she said.

'OK, Mamma.'

'How old are you?' she asked. I watched them both as they began their conversation, my head going back and forth between them.

'Six. And Thomasz is two.'

'Very good. Where you live?'

'London. We from Poland but it is far away now.' He looked a bit sad, and I saw Franceska's eyes darken.

'We go home some time,' she said, quietly.

'Pappa say this is our home,' Aleksy replied.

'Yes, maybe we have two homes,' she said, trying to sound bright. I wanted to tell him what a good idea that was, like me, so I miaowed.

'Ha, the cat makes loud noises.'

'The cat called Alfie.'

'Alfie?' Aleksy repeated it slowly, as if he was trying the sounds out. I wondered at how hard it must be, to have to come and learn a different language, when he can't have been speaking at all for long.

'Yes and maybe he visit a lot?' She looked at me questioningly, and I put my head to one side to try to tell her that, yes, I would visit a lot.

'Mama, what if I don't like school?' Aleksy's big brown eyes filled with tears.

'You will, and it might feel hard at first but you will be OK.'

'OK.'

'We all have to be brave now, Pappa has good job here, and he can make things good for us if we all try hard to it.'

'OK. I miss Pappa.'

'He has to work very much but soon we will see him more. He is doing this for us.'

She went over and sat down next to Aleksy. He had drawn a picture of a house. It wasn't the house that we were in, though. It was a funny looking building, with many windows.

'I miss our old place too,' Franceska said, softly, as she stroked his hair. 'But we will love it here. We just need to be very brave.' And I wondered who she was trying to convince; him or herself.

I was unable to move; watching the mother and son together, I felt like crying myself. I was seeing people trying so hard, learning that life could be really difficult and upsetting for humans as well as cats.

Suddenly, Franceska got up. 'Right, we make some food. Aleksy, come help and you can give to Alfie.'

He cheered up at this idea, and followed his mum into the kitchen. I went, too, and watched as she got some sardines out of the fridge and put them on a plate.

'Yum,' I thought to myself, this was a treat. Salmon, prawns and now sardines. I really had chosen the perfect street to live in.

# Chapter
# Seventeen

Chapter
Seventeen

I hadn't considered the logistics of the flat. There was no cat flap, and only one entrance. There was a small back garden but that was accessed from the side of the house and again was shared with next door. The only way to get out of 22B was to go back through the front door, the way I'd come in. Which wasn't that easy, as the door was shut. I had to figure it out. In the meantime, I ate lots of sardines, drank water and played with Aleksy, who seemed a bit happier now. Although most of his toys weren't exactly designed for cats, we chased a small ball around, which seemed to make him happy. More and more, I understood all the fuss about small children; when they laughed, they made you want to laugh, and their happiness was the most infectious thing I'd encountered. Although, on the flip side, he was quite demanding; not letting me have any time to rest, so I was getting pretty tired. This was a new experience to me, and as much as I was enjoying it, it was exhausting at the same time.

Thomasz, the little one, soon woke up and cried; Franceska went to get him and then brought him back into the living room, where she gave him a bottle filled with milk and sat on the sofa with him. I realised that I really needed to get back to my other homes so I could check on both Claire and Jonathan, and that in order to do so, I would have to make them understand that I needed to leave. After Thomasz finished his drink, I miaowed loudly and then walked down the stairs and stood by the front door.

'Oh goodness, you need getting out,' Franceska said, as she

carried Thomasz downstairs after me. Aleksy followed too. She opened the front door and I turned to face them, to say goodbye properly. I tried to convey with my eyes that I would return, and I purred as well, to tell them I'd had a lovely time. Aleksy leant down and kissed my head. I licked his nose, which made him giggle. Thomasz, who I hadn't heard speak, shouted, 'Cat,' and the other two laughed.

'We must tell Pappa that this his first proper English word,' Franceska said. 'Alfie, you are clever, you gave Thomasz his first English word.' She looked delighted, and I felt very proud. They all stepped outside with me. The sun was still shining brightly and the front lawn was invitingly hot. Just as we all started walking towards the shared gate, the door to 22A opened and Polly emerged. She looked flustered, as she tried to yank a pram out of the small door. I could hear the baby crying from inside.

'Here, I help.' Franceska put Thomasz down and he immediately stood up and walked over to his brother. Franceska pulled the folded pram, which was still far too big, out of the door and put it up in one swift move.

'Thank you,' Polly said. 'I find it hard to manoeuvre it here.' She smiled, a little sadly. 'It's awfully big.'

'Is big. Franceska.' She held out her hand. Polly took it uncertainly. I noticed that she barely touched Franceska's hand before moving hers quickly away.

'Polly. I must just go and get ...' She disappeared back inside and came out carrying Henry and an oversized bag. She laid him in the pram and he started howling again. She rocked the pram a bit as Franceska peered in, and stroked his cheek. Polly looked terrified; the way she'd looked when she first saw me. Maybe she thought Franceska was going to kill the baby too.

'Hello, baby. His name?' Franceska looked at Polly and smiled.

'Henry. Sorry, I've got an appointment with the health visitor and I'm late. Hopefully see you soon, bye.' She turned to shut her front door, but not before I'd sneaked in.

I woke up with no idea where I was. Gradually, I realised I was still in Polly's flat. I padded around, there was no one here still. I was on their large grey sofa, which I must have fallen asleep on – exhausted after all those sardines and playing. I had looked round the flat when Polly shut the door behind me. It was the same size as upstairs, but it wasn't as cosy or comfortable. In addition to the sofa and one armchair, there was a wooden trunk used as a coffee table, a mat thing on the floor with bits dangling from it, which I thought must be Henry's, and a very big TV on the wall. Apart from that, the walls were bare and I wondered whether they didn't have any pictures or just hadn't got round to putting them up.

The biggest bedroom had a big bed, and two small bedside tables but not much else and it was all very white. The smaller bedroom was, however, decorated for a child. There were brightly coloured pictures of animals all over it, and the cot had animals dangling above it. There was a multi-coloured rug on the floor and an abundance of soft toys. It felt as if it was the only colour in an otherwise colourless home. I thought it was quite strange; and had a sense that there was something else going on here, I just didn't know what.

I wondered what time it was – time for me to make a move. But as I looked for a way out, I realised, with a feeling of sudden panic, that I was trapped again, with no obvious escape. There was no one here to help me, so how was I supposed to get out? If only the living room window had been left open a crack, I could have squeezed through it. However, no one in this street ever left their windows open if they weren't home. Panic began to mount; what if they'd gone away? No one knew I was here – was I going to die here? After such a long and treacherous journey, was it really going to come to this? I felt my breathing increase with fear.

Just as I was imagining being left here forever, with no food, water or company, I heard the door open and Matt, Polly and the pram entered. The pram was almost as big as the flat, so Polly had to walk in, followed by Matt, followed by the pram.

'This pram is too big, I can't manoeuvre it,' Polly snapped, almost crying.

'We'll go at the weekend and get something more manageable, babe, it's fine.' Henry was sleeping and they left him in the pram in the hallway and went into the kitchen. The door had slammed shut too quickly for me to get out, plus my interest was pricked now, so I followed them.

'Oh God, how did you get in?' Polly said, looking upset.

'Hi, again,' Matt bent down to stroke me. 'Would you like a drink?' I licked my lips and he laughed as he poured me a saucer of milk.

'Matt, should you be encouraging him?' she asked. 'I don't want him to think he can come here all the time.'

'It's just milk, and anyway, he obviously visits here, so we might as well make him welcome.'

'OK, if you're sure,' Polly sounded unconvinced but she didn't argue. 'What about his owners?'

'Polly, he's only been here twice, so don't worry. He must go back home after he leaves us. Anyway, how was the health visitor?' Matt asked.

'Not like our old one. She was really unfriendly, obviously far too busy to listen to me, and she got rid of me as soon as she could. She knew that Henry was premature, and therefore very delicate, but she just dismissed me.'

'But he is fine now, Polly, you know that don't you?' Matt's voice was gentle; comforting.

'I really couldn't cope. Which is why I sat in the park with Henry until you'd finished work. I didn't know what to do.' Her beautiful face clouded and she burst into tears. Matt looked stricken too.

'It'll get better, Pol, honestly. I'm sorry, but you know I can introduce you to some of the wives of the guys from work and maybe we'll research some baby groups.'

'I don't know if I can. I can't *breathe*, Matt, sometimes I think I can't breathe.' Polly's breathing sounded heavy, as if to illustrate the point. Her eyes were laden with tears; she was clearly shaken. I looked at her and realised that this was serious, there was something wrong with this woman and I could see it, but it seemed Matt couldn't. Or perhaps he just wouldn't. I wasn't sure exactly what was upsetting Polly but instinctively I knew it was something to do with Henry. You hear about it in the cat world, sometimes cats give birth and then have problems bonding with their offspring. I wasn't sure but I felt that maybe that was what I was seeing here. Even if I was wrong, I knew, deep down, that Polly needed help. 'It's just the upheaval, we'll get things sorted.' Just then, a loud wail came from the hallway. Polly looked at her watch.

'It's time for his feed.' She walked towards the pram and I scrambled between her legs, hoping to get to the front door. She looked at me and leant over the pram and awkwardly opened it. I tried to give her my warmest look, but she didn't seem to notice. She was already wearily lifting Henry out of the pram, and then, without a glance in my direction, she shut the door on me. At least I was outside the flat now though.

# Chapter
# Eighteen

Chapter
Eighteen

As I made my way down the street, I wondered who I should go to first. I didn't know what the time was; it was still light, but as Matt had returned from work, I expected the others to be home. I thought I should really check on Jonathan, as he had been in a bit of a state when he left today, and it was his first day in his new job. I felt awful turning up yet again without a present – after all, the dead mouse and bird had helped us to bond, so I decided that I would go out later and get him a little something, just to acknowledge his new job. I found him in the kitchen when I entered through the cat flap (how I wished every house had one).

'Hey, Alfie,' he said, unexpectedly warmly.

I purred.

'Right, well, today wasn't as hideous as I thought it would be. In fact, the shitty job isn't that shitty, and the company was nice. So, to celebrate, I bought us both sushi. I mean, I'm not sure cats eat rice, but I got you some sashimi.' I had no idea what he was talking about but he took some trays out of a brown paper bag and I saw it was fish. Uncooked fish. He laid some out on a plate for me, and put the rest in the fridge. I looked at him questioningly.

'I'm going to the gym, so I'll eat when I get back.' I miaowed in thanks and started to tuck in. I loved this sashimi and I hoped that Jonathan would get it for me again. I felt that being with Jonathan was becoming a fine dining experience and I hoped that he wouldn't suddenly stop and give me the same tinned stuff that Claire did.

'Don't get too used to it,' he said. 'It's only for special occasions.' Hmmm, he really did have a knack of reading my mind.

As I was eating, Jonathan got changed and went to the gym, so I rushed over to see Claire.

Claire was in the living room watching television when I arrived. She didn't look sad any more – maybe this was the new her.

'Hi Alfie, I was just wondering where you were yet again.' She fussed me. I purred with joy. Claire and I had developed our relationship in a way that was harmonious and beneficial to us both. Claire's was still my number one home, not just because it was my first, but also because she and I had established our connection very strongly and quickly. I still didn't always know where I was with Jonathan, although I sensed, secretly, that deep down he liked me. And the number 22 flats were still early days. But Claire and I were family, and I loved her for it.

'Right Alfie, I am going to get changed.' I looked at her questioningly. Where was she going? 'I'm off to the local gym, I've decided that it's time I started taking better care of myself.' She smiled to herself as she made her way upstairs.

What was it with these humans and this gym thing? I wondered if she would go to the same place that Jonathan sometimes went to, and part of me hoped that she wouldn't bump into him. Not yet, anyway, while they both thought I was their cat. That could be awkward.

Instead of worrying about that, I realised that I needed to go for a bit of a walk myself if I was going to work off the day's food. On my way out, I saw Tiger.

'Fancy coming for a walk?' I asked her.

'I was going to have a lazy evening, then maybe go out later,' she said.

'Come on, please. I need to get a present for Jonathan.' In the end, I persuaded her to come with me by promising her first choice of any prey we caught. Women!

We took the scenic route to the local park, meeting some nice cats on the way, and some not so nice dogs. One large dog, probably twice the size of me, wasn't on his lead. He started barking loudly and ran over to me, snarling aggressively and baring his sharp teeth. Tiger, who was more feisty than me, hissed at him, but I tried not to antagonise him. I still felt afraid but now I was better at dealing with danger, so I turned, calling Tiger, ran as fast as my little legs would take me, and shot up the nearest tree. Luckily Tiger was as quick as me and she followed me up. The dog stood at the bottom of the tree, barking furiously until his owner pulled him away. We were exhausted as we caught our breath.

'Alfie, I told you we should have stayed home,' Tiger admonished.

'Yes, but then the running away is actually very good exercise for us,' I retorted.

On the way back, I remembered that I was supposed to be getting a gift for Jonathan. As luck would have it, two nice juicy mice were hanging out by the bins of one of the houses as we made our way back. It was lucky that I wasn't remotely hungry, otherwise I would have been tempted to munch them myself; I saw Tiger polish one of them off almost in one go.

I left the mouse by the front door for him, and then I wandered around aimlessly. I passed some relaxing time with Tiger in her garden, before deciding to go back to Claire's.

Claire was all red and glistening when she got in. It wasn't her best look, and she certainly didn't smell very good, but she seemed happy.

'Goodness me, Alfie, I'm exhausted. But then, I feel better now, doing exercise. They say it's all about endorphins, and I have to say there must be something in it.' As she said this, she picked me up and spun me round, giggling all the time. I tried not to mind, because I knew she was being loving, but she really did need a wash.

'OK, time for me to take a shower.' I felt relieved. I decided that this was a good time for me to give myself a thorough wash too.

# Chapter Nineteen

The next morning I breakfasted with Claire, and then, while she was getting ready for work, I went to see Jonathan.

My morning routine was hectic but I wanted them both to see me before they went to work, so I ate quickly and didn't even have time to clean my whiskers before popping to my next house. It was important to me to give enough attention to both Claire and Jonathan. I wanted them both to think of me as 'their' cat. Jonathan was just about to walk out of the door as I walked in.

'Oh, I wondered where you were. Thanks for the present, but you really shouldn't have. I mean, *really*. I'm sure there are many of us who would be happy to have you rid the street of all mice, but I'd rather they didn't end up on my door mat.' Although he chastised me, I still decided that deep down – perhaps very deep down – he appreciated my gifts. After all, he hadn't thrown me out again, had he? I am a cat and I couldn't bring presents like humans did; Margaret liked to give flowers to her friends, so I was doing the best I could, and perhaps Jonathan understood that better than he let on. I looked at him, licked my lips and miaowed.

'I've left you a bowl with leftovers in from last night. I have to get to work but I'll see you when I get home. Hopefully.' He reached down and tickled me under my chin, which I loved. I let out my loudest purr and he smiled in satisfaction. When he'd left I ignored the food, then gave myself another proper clean and set off to go and see the number 22 flats, reminding myself not to get stuck inside today. After all, there would be delicious food waiting for me on my return here, which I didn't want to go to waste.

I was in luck. It was still early, but Franceska was in the front garden with the boys. The man was there with them too. They looked as if they were about to go out.

'Alfie,' Aleksy shrieked, and ran over to me. I rolled onto my back so he could tickle my tummy.

'Oh, he likes the cat,' the man, Thomasz, said.

'Yes, he like Alfie very much.'

'I have to go to work now, *kochanie*. I'll try to get back before tonight's shift.'

'I love you. I wish it not such a long day for you.'

'I know but that's restaurants for you. Long hours and lots of food.' He laughed as he patted his tummy.

'I'm just miss home, Thomasz.'

'I know, but it gets better.'

'You promise?' she asked.

'Yes *kochanie*. But for now I need to go earn money.'

'English. Is darling.'

'It don't sound right, you are my *kochanie*, no darling.' He laughed, kissed his wife and then both children before he left. Franceska looked tired as she sat on the step and watched the boys playing. I sat next to her.

'At least is sunny. Before I move to England I think it rains always.' I snuggled into her. We sat in companionable silence for a short while. Aleksy was making Thomasz laugh about something and it was such a lovely scene. I felt there was a sadness here too. It seemed that in very different ways, the homes I'd chosen – Claire's, Jonathan's, Polly's, and here – all had this one thing in common; loneliness. And I think that was why I had been so drawn to them. I knew that these people needed my love and kindness; my support and affection. With each passing day my confidence in this increased.

I looked at Polly and Matt's door and realised that the answer was right in front of me. Franceska needed a friend, as did Polly. After all, Claire had been so much happier when she met Tasha. Goodness, it was so simple. I just had to figure out how to do it.

Franceska stood up and rallied the children.

'Come, boys, we go get our shoes and then we go to park.'

They went into the flat. I wondered what I could do, knowing I had to act quickly. I scratched at Polly's door and miaowed very loudly. I yelped, and then I yowled. I'd lose my voice if I didn't get her attention soon.

After a while, she opened the door and looked at me in surprise.

'What's wrong?' she asked, her eyes full of concern. I kept yowling. She bent down. 'Are you hurt?' I carried on, willing Franceska to hurry up. Polly clearly didn't know what to do with me and I felt a little bit guilty for distressing her, but it was for a good cause. 'Oh God, I can't bear it. I don't know what to do. Please, cat, please be quiet.' Polly looked so desperate I almost stopped, but I had to keep going.

Just as I was about to run out of steam, the door opened and Franceska and the boys came out.

'What is this noise?' Franceska asked.

'I don't know what's wrong with him,' Polly replied. I fell silent. I had to have a bit of a lie down to recover my breath. Aleksy came over and tickled me and I snuggled gratefully into him.

'He seems OK now?' Franceska said, looking uncertain.

'But he was making such an awful noise. You'd have thought he was being tortured.' I wanted to say 'thank you'. I was clearly as good as any actor on TV.

'Is he your cat?' Polly asked.

'No, he visits us. I tried to call the number on him collar but it doesn't work.'

'I don't want a cat. I mean, I've got enough to cope with.' Polly suddenly burst into tears. Then a wail started up from inside. 'Oh God, Henry's asleep in his pram. Or he was.' She went inside and came back trying to pull the oversized pram out of the house. Franceska went to help her. When they were both outside, Polly resumed her tears.

'Is OK. Sit down a minute.' Franceska pulled her down to the front step. 'Aleksy, push the pram a bit for baby.' Aleksy did as he was asked, and suddenly the baby stopped crying.

'Mamma, I made him shush,' Aleksy said, gleefully, and even Polly managed to laugh.

'I'm sorry,' she repeated.

'You no sleep?' Franceska asked.

'No. God, never. He – Henry – doesn't sleep. Not through the night, only naps in the day, then he cries. And cries and cries.'

'Is Polly, yes?' Polly nodded. 'Is OK, I know how it is; I have two. Aleksy he never sleep. Thomasz is better.'

'Where are you from?'

'Poland.'

'We're from Manchester.' Franceska looked blank. 'It's in the north of England. My husband, Matt, got a job here and said it was too good not to take. It is a good job, but I miss home.'

'Me too. My husband, same. He is chef and here in London he gets job in very good restaurant. Building better life for us, sure, but is scary and lonely.'

'Yes, it's very lonely. Matt, well, he works long hours even though we've only been here a week. I've taken Henry out to the park, and to see the health visitor – which is nothing like it was at home. I haven't met anyone else.'

'What is a health visitor?'

'Oh, here, when you have a baby, it's someone you visit if you have concerns. In Manchester they were lovely, but here they didn't have time for me. She seemed so busy and when I told her about him not sleeping, she just said that some babies don't sleep.'

'They don't, maybe. But it doesn't sound helpful. Aleksy no sleep, but you know in the end, he was very hungry. He feed all the time. So I buy this night time milk for babies and he drink that and sleep a bit more.'

'Henry's always hungry but I didn't want to give him formula until he was one. I wanted to feed exclusively.'

'What is this?'

'You know, breast only.'

'Oh, me too, but I was going, how do you say it, round the corner.'

'Round the bend. I know. That's exactly how I feel.'

'Someone tells me that the best thing you can do for your child is be capable to looking after them properly. And that means you sleep. So I feed Aleksy in the day and then I give him this at night.'

I was listening intently to their exchange. These two women were fragile in their own ways, Franceska, because she was in a strange country and didn't know anyone, and Polly because she had also moved, and hadn't been sleeping. I could feel that a friendship would begin to form here, and I felt as if I was responsible for it, if I did say so myself. Even if it meant I had to scare Polly half to death in order to do it. These women, both with boys, both lonely, and lost, were perfect for each other. I thought it was about time I reminded them of my presence, so I miaowed.

'Oh Alfie, you still here,' Franceska said. Polly reached out and stroked me half-heartedly. It was a very limp stroke. 'He was in our flat the other day. I was worried, I heard that cats can kill babies.' I blanched again; I really didn't appreciate her telling people that she thought I was a killer.

'Oh, I never hear that. I like the cats. This one very smart too.'

'How can you tell?'

'He kind of introduced us, yes? I say we all go to the shop now to buy some milk for baby and then maybe we walk to the park and Henry he will sleep, yes?'

'Oh, that would be so nice. Thank you, really, I'd love some female company. And you're right, we'll try the formula. I almost feel I have nothing left to lose.'

'Good. I need the company too. My boys are lovely but I need the grown up. Sorry my English is bad.'

'Not at all, it's great! Blimey, I can't speak any other languages.' And as they chatted on, I could sense a friendship had been sealed.

I watched them all get ready to go off. Thomasz had been reluctantly strapped into a pushchair, Aleksy walked next to it, Polly pushed her giant pram, and Henry was still not crying. Polly was so tall, thin and blonde and Franceska was what I would call sturdy. She wasn't fat but whereas Polly looked as if she would fall over if I so much as brushed her legs, Franceska looked like she could withstand any storm. But she was very lovely with her dark, short gleaming hair, and brown eyes, which lit up when she smiled. She had one of the nicest smiles I had ever seen.

Before they left the garden, they stopped and said good-bye to me. Aleksy asked me to come back soon, and I purred, because I would come and see the lovely boy; I felt that he would be my friend.

They definitely looked like opposites as they started down the road together; one so fair, one so dark, one tall, one short, but I knew instinctively that they would fit together, and I did feel that, however unwittingly, I had helped with this. I didn't mean to boast but I did feel that credit should be given to me.

I was intrigued by these women's stories and I really hoped to spend more time with them, together. I liked the idea of us all hanging out on the front lawn, I would never be bored with that. And my friendship with Aleksy and Thomasz would grow because every little boy deserved a cat. It was a good day all round. Friendships had begun, and who knew where they would take us?

# Chapter
# Twenty

Being a doorstep cat was not for the faint-hearted.

As the weeks passed, I was very busy as I tried to juggle my four homes. I was beginning to learn that being a cat with four families wasn't as easy as I had first thought it would be. It was rewarding, but hard work. I was starting to devise a schedule, but it was proving tricky.

Claire was becoming more relaxed with every passing day and I knew this was the healing process, because of course, I'd been through it myself. I could see in her what I felt in me.

Not that you ever become completely healed, you understand. There will always be a part of you that is still healing, still hurting, but that becomes a part of your character and you learn to live with it. That's what I think happens, anyway, because that's how it feels to me. But I loved to see Claire smiling and looking so much better. She was putting on a bit of weight too, she didn't look so much like a scrawny sparrow any more. She had more colour in her cheeks and she was getting better looking by the day.

There had been a lot of women at Jonathan's house. Although they were not appearing quite as frequently any more, there was still an alarming number, it seemed to me. But to his credit, now that he was working, he was more sensible with his time; going to bed early and either working in the evenings, or going to the gym. He was looking better for it too; he was quite handsome to start with, but he was even more so now he didn't scowl quite so much.

I had been splitting my evenings between Claire and

Jonathan so far. So long as I saw them both at some point, they seemed happy. On the whole, Claire would arrive home from work earlier than Jonathan, so we would dine together, and we would hang out for a bit. We cuddled while she read a book, watched TV, or chatted on the phone with a glass of wine, and then I'd take that as my cue to visit Jonathan.

I would head off to greet him on his return from work. He often worked in the evenings, which wasn't much fun for me, so I had a new routine at night time. I'd go out for a long walk or run to get some exercise. I had put on weight, what with all the extra meals, but I was still far from being as fat as the ginger cat a few doors down, who could barely move and would easily be outmanoeuvred by any mouse.

I would go and see Tiger, and we would sometimes hang out with some of the neighbourhood cats; even the mean ones seemed to be used to me, now. After socialising, I would decide where to sleep. I alternated between Claire's and Jonathan's, but the problem was that both of them seemed to quite like to see me first thing in the morning. If I slept at Claire's, I would wake at the same time as her and scoot over to go and see Jonathan before he left for work, and vice versa. It could be exhausting, but I tried my best to fit everyone in. Keeping them happy was far from an easy task though, and my life was incredibly complex.

During the day, when Claire and Jonathan were at work, I would go to the number 22 flats. This was perfect for me. I would often stand at Franceska's door and miaow, and after a while, either she or Aleksy would let me in. They would give me fish, normally sardines, but the best thing was that Aleksy would play with me, and we would have so much fun. I would roll onto my back and he would tickle my tummy, which had become my new favourite game. The household was happy for the most part. Sometimes when Thomasz was napping and Aleksy was playing I would find Franceska in the kitchen, leaning against the counter and looking as if she was miles away. I knew she was missing her home still, although she was the most resilient of the adults I spent time with because she mainly hid it, and made sure her house was full of laughter. But I often thought her head was sometimes in Poland, even if her body was here; the way that when I had lived on the streets, my head and heart were far away, with Margaret and Agnes, even though I didn't quite know where they were.

One weekend, I was over at Franceska's flat. Claire had gone out for the day with Tasha, Jonathan had gone to meet friends for something he called 'brunch', so I went to Franceska's house and her husband, the big Thomasz, let me in. They all made their usual fuss of me and he seemed like a very nice man. He played with the children, while Franceska cooked a big lunch for them all. He was very affectionate, both with her and the boys and I could see that although she found life hard sometimes, she was surrounded by love. It made me feel better because she deserved it very much. It was such a warm, loving family, it tickled my whiskers.

Sometimes I saw Polly and baby Henry with Franceska. As it was summer, they would often be on the front lawn. They had taken to having coffee together while the boys all sat on a blanket. Well, Henry would lie on the blanket, but he didn't cry as much and he seemed to find the older boys' presence calming. They would shake rattles at him, and they even managed to make him giggle quite a lot. Polly still seemed very uptight though, and I rarely saw her smile. There was something unnerving about the way she was.

Not only did the women look different from each other, but also as mothers they couldn't be further apart. Franceska was so calm with her boys, and they were such happy children. Polly was wound up tightly and she held Henry as if he was made of glass. She seemed so awkward, even when she was feeding him, and she seemed to cry as much as Claire had in the early days. Franceska kept saying it was tiredness, and that was why she was so emotional, but I wondered if it really could be that. Since giving the baby the formula he was apparently sleeping more. Not a huge amount, but enough to make a difference, so surely she should be better?

Franceska would often take both of them into her flat where they would feed the boys, and she would try to get food into Henry. He seemed happier when he was there, as well. He didn't cry as much and he smiled and laughed; I wondered sometimes if Polly noticed. She was so sad and I didn't know if she even registered half of what was going on. I was more worried about her than I was about any of the others, but despite that, I had decided to stop going to her flat – it just wasn't a good idea. Polly tolerated me, but she still treated me with suspicion, although I got the feeling that she needed me more than my other families. I just didn't quite know why.

I watched these humans, who were all so different in many ways to my Margaret. Not only were they considerably younger, and less wrinkly, but they were unlike her in other ways too. Claire was blossoming, and had almost totally changed from the thin, shaggy, crying woman I first met. She still had moments of sadness, normally when it was just the two of us, but they were getting fewer and fewer. Jonathan was still complex, but he was also becoming happier; I think it wasn't just the job, but the new friends he was making at work. Not just women with big boobs and shiny hair. However, I still thought he was too solitary. He didn't have people round to the big, empty house apart from the women. He did go out a bit, about as much as Claire, but still, he had moments of looking as if he had lost something. It was how I'd looked when I woke up every day just after Agnes died. I would wake up and before I remembered what had happened I would look for her. It seemed that Jonathan was looking for someone who wasn't there, too.

Franceska was more like Margaret than the others; she seemed so solid and sensible, and although she was obviously missing home, she seemed the most sorted out of everyone. Polly was the opposite. So fragile that she looked as if she would break at any time, although sometimes I wondered if she was already broken.

Each of them needed me in their own ways and I vowed every day that I would be there, and I would help them all.

I had survived, and now I had to help others survive, too.

The problem was that my lifestyle was so busy I couldn't be in four places at once, but if my plan was to work I really had to be.

'It's hard work,' I told Tiger.

'Having four homes would be. Four sets of humans to keep happy.' Tiger shuddered. 'My one home is enough for me, although I understand.'

'I can't be alone again. I have to make sure that there will always be someone to take care of me, Tiger.'

'I know. And anyway most cats think loyalty is overrated.'

'But I'm fiercely loyal; just to four different families. I have to learn to spread myself thinly.'

'Alfie, stop being dramatic. My owners are married, and

although they don't have children, if anything happens to them … Well, before meeting you, I hadn't even thought about it.'

'I hope what happened to me doesn't happen to you, but you're lucky because if it does, you'll have me to take care of you.'

'Thanks Alfie, you're a good friend.'

'Tiger, I wouldn't want anyone, cat or human, to go through what I've been through. I've learnt the importance of compassion the hard way. I know what it's like when there is none. And although I was lucky to find some along my journey and in my homes now, I know how incredibly crucial it is to our survival. For all of us.'

'You'll never be alone again now,' Tiger pointed out, kindly.

It was true, compassion needed others. That was my lesson. It was through the compassion of other cats as well as other humans that I survived after Margaret died. It made me realise, life was a funny thing; as much as I would welcome being reunited with Agnes and Margaret, there was a part of me that wanted to survive, to carry on living, and I didn't understand it.

# Chapter
# Twenty-One

I was asleep at Claire's, on her sofa in the living room. I wasn't necessarily banned from sleeping on the sofa, but Claire did try, nicely, to encourage me to use my cat bed. However, the evening sun had been streaming through the window, making the spot I settled on deliciously warm and pretty irresistible – just what I needed after a difficult afternoon. I'd come home from Franceska's house feeling hungry. I'd played with Aleksy for hours but there had been no sardines, no drink, nothing. Franceska hadn't been as cheerful as normal; she seemed distracted, and although I tried to spend a bit of time with her on her own, she didn't seem to notice me. I felt a little bit upset at being ignored. I knew that humans had problems, but that shouldn't be an excuse for ignoring me – after all, I was there to help her when things were difficult! And there was no sign or sound of Polly and Henry. They returned home just as I was leaving, along with Matt. He was pushing the pram and she seemed a little bit more relaxed for once, but they were deep in conversation and they didn't seem to notice me. It seemed I had become invisible to the adults of the number 22 flats.

And that was just the start of it. As afternoon turned into evening, things got worse.

Claire had been at home getting ready to go out, so although she had put some cat food and milk out for me, she didn't have time for a chat, or any affection at all. She seemed very happy, and preoccupied with getting dressed up. She was wearing a very nice black dress and she put some high-heeled shoes by the front door. I'd never seen her wear heels that high, not even for work.

She also spent ages on her hair, and putting lots of stuff on her face.

When she had finished, I didn't think she looked like my Claire any more.

'Alfie, don't wait up, I'm going out with the girls,' she said, smiling, but she didn't pick me up or stroke me; she probably thought I would mess up her dress with my cat hair. As if I would! I felt a little hurt again, although I knew it was selfish as I wanted her to be happy, so I tried to be glad for her. But I didn't purr or even raise my whiskers for her when she left; I really did feel very down in the mouth.

Bored and a bit lonely, I went to Jonathan's but there was no sign of him. He hadn't come back from work it seemed, and he hadn't left me any food either. My empty breakfast dishes were still on the floor, just as I'd left them. Although I had still had enough to eat, I felt a bit disappointed, not just in the lack of food, but also the lack of attention.

It made me realise that cats always need to have their wits about them. Just because I was no longer a homeless cat didn't mean that I could take anything for granted. People were far from stable and reliable. Of course I wasn't trying to exaggerate, I knew they were still there to take care of me, but I also needed to be more self-reliant and also perhaps a little less sensitive. After all, I'd been a street cat for a while, so there was no reason for me to have reverted to being quite so soft.

But I still was. And I felt a little bit lost. I went for a walk, but I didn't feel like making small talk with the other cats, not even Tiger. I was feeling sorry for myself. I wandered around Jonathan's house, including the rooms that he never used, but that wasn't much fun. I thought about hunting for a gift for him but I couldn't be bothered; why reward him for his neglect? I felt a little bit sad as I decided to go back to Claire's, and that's when I fell asleep on the warm spot on the sofa.

I was woken up by the sound of a key turning in the front door and giggling. I looked outside, where it was pitch black. Claire came into the living room, being held up by a man I'd never seen. I immediately stood up and raised my tail in suspicion, ready to rescue her, as a light flicked on.

'Oh Alfie's here, Alfie my lovely,' Claire's words sounded funny and slurry as I darted out of her way. I knew she was drunk. She wasn't quite as bad, or mean, as the drunk people I had met on the street but she definitely shared common traits with them. If I let her pick me up, she would probably drop me, knowing my luck.

'Right, well, Claire, you're home safe and sound, so I better go.' The man shuffled a bit, looking as if he wasn't quite sure what to do.

'Nooo Joe, stay for coffee.' She burst out laughing, as if this was the funniest thing she had ever said. I didn't think it was, though.

'Thanks, but I'd better go, Claire. Honestly, you'll thank me in the morning.' The man looked quite nice, but he had hair the same colour as the fat ginger cat down the road.

She flung herself at him, literally, and they both fell backwards onto the sofa. I bolted swiftly, only narrowly escaping getting squashed. Claire giggled again and Joe seemed to struggle a bit to free himself from her grip.

'Claire, you're a bit drunk,' he persisted; he sounded a bit exasperated. It looked like that was an understatement. 'I really ought to go but I promise I'll call you.'

'Please don't go,' she slurred, but he got up, kissed her on her cheek and let himself out. 'Oh God, I'm such a loser,'

Claire cried as soon as the door closed. Alarmingly, she started sobbing like the old days. Then, instead of going to bed, she just curled up on the sofa and started snoring.

Although I had seen this behaviour, I had no idea what to do, and actually there was nothing I could do but curl up next to her and snore along with her.

She woke up the next morning, still on the sofa, and she really looked a mess.

'Oh my God,' she said, clutching her hair. 'What on earth did I do?' She looked at me. 'Oh Alfie, I'm sorry, I hope you're OK?' She tried to get up. 'My head is agony.' She fell back again. 'Oh God, oh God,' she repeated, clutching her head as she moaned. I started miaowing, to let her know I was hungry.

'Oh God, Alfie, can you keep it down, you sound like a fog horn.' I didn't know what that was, so I continued miaowing, and I didn't understand why she was like this. If this was the result of being drunk, then why on earth did humans do it?

Eventually she got up again and went to the kitchen. She drank a glass of water and then another one straight away. She went to the fridge and got some food out for me, which made her turn a funny colour as she put it on a plate.

'Oh no, I think I'm going to be sick,' she said, as soon as she'd put it down. She rushed off. As I ate my breakfast, I didn't really know what to think. It wasn't a work day for Claire, which was probably lucky, as she looked dreadful. She returned looking pale, although she did have the remnants of the previous night's make-up dotted around her face. She also smelt terrible (admittedly not as bad as the street drunks), although I accept that I have a heightened sense of smell, being a cat.

'Oh Alfie, did that guy, Joe, come back here last night?' I

miaowed, hoping she would interpret that as a yes. 'I just can't remember. Oh no, he must hate me. I bet he can't stand me now, and I quite liked him. Oh God, at my age I should know better. I am so embarrassed.' I yelped really loudly. The last thing I ever wanted was to lose her now.

'Not literally,' she said, as if she understood me. 'Sorry Alfie, but I'm going to bed and I think I'm going to stay there for the rest of the day.' She left the room. I looked after her wistfully. My humans were complicated, that was for sure. I was beginning to feel as if I would never fully get to understand any of them.

I went to Jonathan's, as Claire was clearly not going to be any fun at all today, but he still wasn't home. I wondered if he'd come home and then gone out early but my breakfast dishes were still on the floor; he clearly hadn't thought about feeding me at all. I fleetingly wondered if I should worry, but then Jonathan wasn't the sort of man you worried about. If I could take care of myself then he certainly could. But I didn't like the fact that he hadn't been home at all since he left for work in the morning. And I particularly didn't like the fact that he hadn't given me a second thought, otherwise he wouldn't have made me miss two meals. I wondered what I could do to convey my anger to him.

I was about to give up on him and leave. Obviously I couldn't reward his behaviour with another gift, so I thought that if I walked out on him the way he walked out on me, then maybe he would understand what it felt like. But as I was about to head out, I heard the door open and in he walked, in his work clothes, but looking quite fresh regardless. Nothing like Claire, that was for sure.

'Alfie, sorry,' he said, petting me and smiling at me in a

way I hadn't quite seen him do before. 'I hope you're not too hungry – I didn't expect to be gone so long.' I miaowed angrily, in a way that said he certainly wasn't forgiven, and yes, I was expecting him to be there for me; after all, he didn't know I had already eaten.

'Oh, Alfie, you're a man of the world. You know how it is when you get lucky,' he winked. I blinked, then looked at him through narrowed eyes. I didn't know how it was. I certainly wasn't that sort of cat. He laughed.

'If I didn't know better, I'd say you disapproved.' He laughed again. His phone beeped. He read something and smiled. I wondered if he was still drunk like Claire had been last night, because he wasn't himself. He definitely seemed happy, but maybe a little bit crazy. 'Sorry, of course you're hungry. I'll get you some food.' He looked a bit puzzled as he picked up my empty plates and then he fetched me some prawns. They might be one of my favourite things but I wasn't going to be won over that easily.

All the while I ate, he played with his phone. He would type something, it would beep and he'd smile and type something else. I actually found it all irritating; in my mood I would have preferred to dine in peace.

'Alfie,' he said finally. 'I like the woman I went out with last night. I've known her for a while, although not well, but I saw her again last week. Anyway, she's attractive, funny, smart and has a good job. I actually think I may be a bit "in like" with her.' I refused to look at him and concentrated on my dwindling prawns.

'Oh come on, you can't be mad at me forever. Surely you can be happy for me?' I felt my fur prick up as I wanted to tell him that I surely couldn't, if it meant I was going to be forgotten about. I could really, if it meant he wasn't sad any more, although I wasn't ready to let him know that! 'Look, this is why I didn't want a cat. I'm free and easy and if I want to stay out, I should be able to. I don't mind when you stay out all night, for God's sake. I'm a grown up, Alfie.' Still I didn't turn round. 'Oh, Alfie, just get over it. Next time I'm going out I'll bring her back here.' I turned around, but I didn't give him a smile. 'And why the hell am I apologising to a bloody cat?' Jonathan looked bemused.

I gave him an indignant look, then I stalked out of the cat flap. But as soon as I stood outside, I realised it was raining. I hadn't thought about the weather, being too cross to do so, but what a predicament I'd put myself in. Claire was asleep, Jonathan was in the dog house, and so I had no alternative but to get wet, which I hated, and walk down the street to the flats at number 22.

Feeling extremely disapproving of both Claire and Jonathan – Margaret had certainly never got up to such antics – I thought that perhaps it was time to step up my charm offensive with both Franceska and Polly. Maybe they would be more reliable.

As luck would have it, I struck gold. Matt, Polly's husband, was pushing the pram into the house as I arrived, allowing me to sneak in.

'Oh, hello Alfie,' he said, and I felt quite chuffed, both that he spoke to me and that I was in the dry. He took his shoes off and left the pram just inside the door. I purred.

'Shush,' he said, quietly. 'I've just got Henry off to sleep. Polly is having a much-needed lie-in. Come in and I'll get you a towel to dry you off and give you some milk.' I followed him into their small, but very neat, kitchen. He grabbed a tea towel and rubbed me down which was very nice, before pulling some milk out of the fridge and filling the kettle. I felt companionship developing between us as he quietly put some milk in a bowl for me, giving me a gentle pat. I lapped the milk as quietly as I could while Matt made himself a drink. He took it through to the living room and I joined him. We sat, side by side, on the sofa. He picked up a book to read and I just sat, quietly, showing him that I was able to be a good cat. I curled up, and after a while I started dozing off. I was roused a short while later by Polly appearing.

'How long did I sleep for? Where's Henry?' She sounded panicked.

'It's fine, darling. He's asleep in the pram and you probably got a couple of hours' kip.'

'But doesn't he need feeding?'

'He had breakfast, and it's not lunchtime yet. Pol, he's over six months so he can probably start having more regular feeding times.'

'That's what the health visitor said. And Franceska.'

'So they're probably right, then. Can I make you a cup of tea?'

'Thanks, that would be lovely.' Matt got up and Polly sat down next to me.

'Hello, cat,' she said stiffly. I tried to raise my eyes; she knew my name. 'Sorry, Alfie,' she corrected. I was sure that I was getting quite good at communicating with these humans, but then I was getting a lot of practice. She reached over and lightly touched my fur. I stayed still. Polly seemed afraid of me, but then, she seemed afraid of everything. One observation I had made was that she was definitely afraid of her baby. She seemed terrified of tiny Henry.

Matt returned with the tea and put it on the coffee table

in front of her. He picked me up and sat down, putting me on his lap.

'I hope that Henry isn't allergic to his fur,' Polly said.

'Of course he isn't. Mum had a cat and we were round there all the time.'

'Oh yes, I'd forgotten,' Polly replied. She looked vague. Matt's brow creased and he didn't look happy.

'Polly, are you OK? I mean really? I know this move has been a huge upheaval and I didn't realise I'd be working so much straight away, but I'm worried about you.'

'I'm fine.' She looked around the room with an expression on her face that seemed to say she had no idea where she was. It was still quite bare, the same as when they moved in. Apart from the sofa, chair and trunk table, the room was quite sparse. Even with the baby mat and toys on the floor it still didn't seem like a home, nothing like next door. 'It's just hard and I'm tired,' she continued. 'I'm tired and I'm homesick and although I have Franceska now, I do feel lonely. I miss my family.' It was the most I'd heard her say, even to Franceska.

'I'll do anything to help you,' Matt said. 'Maybe we can go home soon, would you like that? Or if you really want to, you and Henry can go and see your mum for a week. I could drive you up on Sunday and pick you up the following weekend.' He looked a bit pleased with himself.

'So you want to get rid of us, do you?' Her voice was filled with panic.

'No, I'd miss you both, of course, but I just thought you'd like to spend some time with your mum.' Polly glared at Matt but further conversation was interrupted by Henry's loud wails.

'I'll feed him.'

'Do you want me to make up some baby rice or formula?'

Matt asked. He sounded very sad; defeated even.

'No, my breasts are hurting. I'll feed him.' She disappeared and I could hear Henry's wails all the way to the bedroom. I heard the door close and then it went quiet. Matt sighed, and looked as if he was far away. It was similar to the way that Franceska looked sometimes. He started stroking me absently, and although I knew he was thinking about other things, I enjoyed it all the same.

After a while, Polly returned with Henry. She put him down on the mat and he started grabbing at his toys.

'We need to encourage him to start sitting up on his own,' she said.

'OK, well I'll put some cushions behind him.' Matt started arranging cushions, he looked grateful for something to do. He then propped Henry up, coaxing him to try to sit by rattling toys in front of him. Henry liked this game and started giggling. Matt laughed, and even Polly smiled. I wished they would take a photo so they could look at it and remember that they were a happy family; because for that moment they looked like one.

'Right, Pol, shall we go and get ourselves a smaller push-chair, so we can get rid of that bloody monster truck?' Matt suggested, after Henry had given up with the sitting game and was lying on his back again, studying his feet.

'Yes, we can walk down to that shop Franceska and I found the other day.' She perked up a bit.

'Shall I take him in the sling?' Polly nodded and they started to busy themselves getting ready.

I took this as my cue to leave. I watched them walk down the street and then I miaowed really loudly outside Franceska's house. But there was no sign of anyone and there were no lights on in the house. It looked like they had gone out. It seemed everyone had somewhere to go but me.

So instead, I went to visit Tiger. The community I was building wasn't just made up of my new families, it also included fellow cats. Now, at last, if ever I was in need, I had a support network to fall back on and it was growing stronger by the minute. Not that I would ever be in trouble again, but just in case …

'So what do you want to do?' Tiger asked.

'Let's go to the pond by the park and look at our reflections.' It was one of my favourite new pastimes. Tiger and I would stand on the bank, as close to the pond as we dared go, and we would look at ourselves in the water. We looked so funny as the water distorted us; it was a very pleasant way to spend the afternoon.

We then explored the back gardens in the street, jumping fences and sheds and having a fun old time without any of the nonsense I'd been subjected to lately.

'Oh, look at that funny small dog,' Tiger pointed out. We hissed loudly at him, from our vantage point on a fence, and he yapped, running around in circles in his back garden. It was good, innocent fun. I enjoyed being with Tiger, she was good company today; very compliant, not too loud and generally entertaining to be with.

# Chapter Twenty-Two

As I entered Jonathan's house one evening a few days later, I was struck by a delicious smell. I found Jonathan in the kitchen, doing something I had never seen him do before; cooking. There was a bottle of wine open on the side and he had a bottle of his beer next to him.

'Hi Alfie. Have you forgiven me yet?' he asked. I purred. I hadn't seen much of him over the past couple of days but I had forgiven him, on the proviso that I would get a good dinner out of it. As much as I liked the others, he gave me the best food. He went to the fridge and took out an open packet of salmon. He dished some out for me and smiled warmly. I narrowed my eyes at him; there was something different about him but I couldn't put my paw on it. Instead, I ate and then took a place on the windowsill in the kitchen, where I could watch him and look outside as well.

I enjoyed watching him cook. He had changed his clothes, and looked nice in a white shirt and pair of jeans. He also smelt good. He whistled as he cooked, and he had this new energy about him; what a cat would liken to having a spring in their step.

The doorbell rang and Jonathan seemed to bounce towards the front door. I waited. After a while he returned with a woman in tow and I understood his mood. She was tall and slim, with long auburn hair. She was wearing jeans and a white shirt, dressed a bit like him, actually. She didn't look like the type of women I'd seen here before, that was for sure. She was attractive but not like his other women. I guess she was more

179

groomed and not falling out of her clothes. 'Philippa, can I get you a glass of wine?'

'That would be lovely, thank you.' Her voice was very posh.

'Red or white?'

'Um, red please.' He gestured to her to take a seat at the kitchen table and delivered a glass of wine to her.

'Thank you.'

I was still on the windowsill, but she hadn't looked at me. I miaowed to let her know I was here.

'Is that a cat?' she asked.

'What?' I thought. 'Of course I'm a cat. What a stupid question.'

'Yes, that's Alfie,' Jonathan replied.

'You don't strike me as a cat man,' she said dryly, and again I felt insulted.

'He kind of came with the house. And although I didn't think I wanted any kind of pet, let alone a cat, I'm really fond of him.' I preened myself. Take that, you mean woman; Jonathan really did like me.

'I don't like cats,' she said. I couldn't believe my ears; I wanted to scratch her but I knew that was the wrong thing to do. 'Don't see the point of them at all.' I waited for Jonathan to step in and defend me.

'I suppose if I had a snake or a lizard, that would seem more manly,' he joked.

'Or even a dog. But a cat?'

'He's all right, you'll get used to him, I did. More wine?'

I was so upset that I jumped off the windowsill and hissed as loudly as I could, before stalking out.

'Look, you've upset him now,' Jonathan said, laughing rather than sounding cross, like he should have done.

'He's a bloody cat, for God's sake.' Those were the last words I heard as I strode out of the house.

I spent the next few evenings with Claire, who hadn't been herself since the whole drunken incident. She still went to work every day, but she looked sad when she came home in the evenings and although I didn't know why, I paid her extra attention for a few days. I didn't know exactly what she needed but I made sure she knew that I was there for her. That I would do anything to make sure she was OK.

Just as we were having supper together, her phone rang. She looked at the screen, blinked and then answered it.

'Hello.' She looked a bit shocked. 'Oh Joe, hi.' There was a pause. I couldn't hear what he was saying. 'I am so sorry about the other night, I was so drunk and I don't normally drink like that.' No, she didn't, in all fairness. She might have liked her wine but I hadn't seen her that bad before.

They chatted for a bit longer, and as they did, a huge smile began to form on her face. When she hung up, she picked me up and cuddled me as if I was a rag doll.

'Oh Alfie, I didn't mess up. He's coming here for dinner tomorrow night. Goodness, I really thought I'd made a fool of myself. Oh God, what am I going to wear? What am I going to cook? I haven't had a date for years. Years! Oh, crikey. I have to call Tash.' She jumped up and danced around the room a bit.

I was trying to help but it seemed that a phone call from a man she barely knew could do more than I ever could! Humans. They were definitely, absolutely, beyond even my advanced comprehension.

I stopped to watch Tiger trying and failing to catch birds as I made my way to Jonathan's. I'd left Claire on the phone to Tasha; she was full of excitement. As I continued on to Jonathan's, I wondered what I would find there. As I walked through the cat flap the kitchen was clean, but empty. I went into the living room and there he was, on the phone.

'That's OK, I enjoyed cooking for you.' There was a pause. 'I'm frantic at work too but how about Wednesday?' Another pause. 'Brilliant, I'll book a restaurant, see you then, Philippa.' He hung up and seemed to notice me.

'Alfie, my mate,' he said, affectionately scooping me up onto his lap. 'I am feeling very happy right now. I think I told you that I knew Philippa years ago, before I went to Singapore. We were both with other people, actually she was living with one of my old work colleagues. So imagine how I felt when I bumped into her and we're both single! Honestly, having a cat might not be very manly, but I'm pretty sure you're my good luck charm.' He laughed and then went to get ready for his 'gym'.

I felt like a bit of a yo-yo as I headed back to Claire's. She was sitting at the kitchen table writing something.

'Hello, babes,' she said, and I almost looked around until I realised she was talking to me. I sat on the chair next to her and wished I could read as she scribbled away. The doorbell rang and she went to the door, returning with Tasha.

'Thank you so much for coming round, honestly, you are such a good friend.'

'Not really, I should have insisted you came home with me, rather than leaving you that night.' Tasha gave me a cuddle.

'I was so drunk.'

'I was, too, which is why I left you with the others. Anyway, it's all OK. Joe obviously likes you, you like him, and you have a date tomorrow.'

'I feel like a giggly teenager. But I'm also terrified. Oh, God. Anyway, now that you're here, this is what I was going to cook.' They both looked at her list. 'I have no idea if he likes Italian food but homemade lasagne and a green salad … I know it's not very exciting, but it should work, don't you think?'

'I think it's great, and he won't care about the food when he sees what you're wearing.'

'But I don't know what I'm wearing!' Claire protested.

'Come upstairs, you soon will.' They both giggled.

I followed them into Claire's bedroom where Claire and I plonked ourselves down on the bed and Tasha opened the wardrobe and began trawling through her clothes.

'What do you feel like wearing?' she asked.

'Well I thought a dress, because I look better in dresses but then, I'm at home and I don't want to look as if I'm trying too hard.'

'Jeans. I think jeans and a sexy top would be best.' She started pulling tops out.

'I think if you get the jeans and the top right, you'll give off the right message. Besides, your figure is to die for now. He'll be putty in your hands.'

'I hope so. I really did like him.'

'I can't really remember him, although he did have red hair, didn't he?'

'Yes, he has lovely hair and was funny too.'

'Well, you deserve some fun.'

'I do, don't I?' Claire giggled.

'Right, try this on and we'll see how you look.'

I stayed on the bed, watching the fashion parade, as the women laughed. It was nice to hear, after seeing Claire in despair again the past few days, but it worried me. If a man could do that to her, one she hardly knew, was she ready to date again? I might not be an expert, but I had seen how Claire was when she first moved here and now she'd had a mini-relapse. I would go so far as to suggest she was still very unstable. I needed to keep an eye on her.

They finally settled on an outfit and made their way downstairs.

'Do you fancy a cup of tea?' Claire offered.

'No, thanks, I better get back. Dave has decided that we need to eat dinner together tonight.'

'Oh God, sorry for dragging you over here.'

'Don't be silly. I enjoyed it. Anyway, I'll see you at work, but just in case I don't get to speak to you on your own, remember; a date is meant to be fun. He might not be "the one", but you just need to enjoy yourself. And remember it is just a date.'

'I know, I need to not take it so seriously. It's early days, but I'm trying.'

After Tasha left, Claire snuggled up on the sofa and I joined her.

'I'm sorry I've been such a mess lately. I love you, Alfie.' And I rewarded her with my best cat smile. 'Things are looking up, you know.' I purred in agreement. I really hoped that was true, but somehow I just wasn't convinced.

# Chapter Twenty-Three

Chapter
Twenty-
Three

I was running late. I had to bolt from number 22B, where Franceska and Aleksy had been dressing me up and taking photos, creating hours of fun for them and Thomasz, who couldn't stop giggling, and hours of humiliation for me. They'd put hats and sunglasses on me, scarves and anything else that they could find. Then they'd taken photos with Franceska's phone and laughed all over again. I was surely above all this? But they didn't seem to think so and short of running away in a huff, I had to put up with it. Luckily, I loved the family enough to know that one day I would forgive them (probably tomorrow), but only on the proviso that I got sardines again.

The dress-up game took most of the afternoon. I didn't see Polly or Henry at all but I couldn't think about that because I wanted to be home to see Claire, and make sure she was happy before her dinner with Joe.

I rushed through the cat flap and came face to leg with her. She looked great and the food smelt amazing as I rubbed her leg in greeting.

'Oh there you are, I was beginning to worry. Do you want your supper? Quickly, Joe is due any minute.' She seemed flustered as she dished some food into my bowls; she now had a special mat on the floor for them. I ate my supper quietly, and then I gave myself a very thorough clean. I wanted to look my best for Joe too.

Although Claire was busy cooking, washing up my dishes and playing with her hair, she wasn't stressed, she seemed more excited than anything. I felt excited too. When the doorbell went, we both jumped. She fluffed her hair again and I ran my paw over my fur, and then I followed her to answer the door.

He was standing behind a huge bouquet of flowers, but I still recognised him from the other night; you couldn't forget that red hair.

'Joe, come in.' He walked in the door, kissed Claire on each cheek and handed her the flowers. He also produced a bottle of wine.

'Thank you so much, they're beautiful. Come through to the living room and I'll pour some wine. Are you OK with white?'

'Lovely. Don't worry; I remember where the living room is!' He winked at her. I tried not to feel indignant that he had ignored me, so I followed them both through into the room. He sat on the sofa and I sat on the floor in front of him.

'Did you meet Alfie the other night?' she asked him.

'Not that I remember. Hi, Alfie,' he said, reaching out to stroke me. 'Cute cat,' he said, smiling. But I knew he didn't mean it – I could tell. Firstly, he nearly sat on me the other night, so I knew full well he'd seen me. And secondly, you can tell how people feel about you from the way they stroke you. Of course there are other ways of telling, but if someone really likes cats, they stroke you as if they mean it. I guess it's like the cat equivalent of a handshake. I've watched some people take a hand and give it a good solid shake, whilst others barely touch it. Joe, with his half-hearted stroke, definitely didn't mean it and I felt sad. Not only did Jonathan's friend overtly dislike me, but Joe secretly did too. I wasn't doing very well at all.

As if to prove me right, when Claire went to pour the drinks he looked around the room without giving me another glance. I tried to approach him, but he looked at me with mean eyes.

'Get, cat,' he said, quietly. Deeply insulted, I slunk away and went to sit under the chair. I might as well observe the evening, as I obviously wasn't going to be invited to participate in any way.

Claire appeared to be happy and he seemed charming with her, but I knew immediately he was faking things, and not only because of his behaviour towards me. He made her laugh, although I couldn't understand why; nothing he said was remotely funny.

'I love working in advertising,' he said. 'The creative part and dealing with clients. I particularly enjoy the face to face aspect of it.'

'I guess so, although in my job I prefer it when I don't have to deal with the clients, I often find it easier to get the job done.'

'I hear you, Claire. But I find it challenging. You know, when you get a really good idea and the client hates it, but you really want it and you finally persuade them. There's no buzz like it.'

'I guess that you are more suited to it than me. But anyway, since being in London I'm getting used to it.'

'Different from Exeter, though.'

'Very. But you know, I'm really happy I made the move.'

'Let's drink to that. New start, new friends.' They clinked their glasses.

'Right, new friend, let's sit down for dinner. And hope that I don't poison you.'

I sat under the table while they ate, quietly eavesdropping and totally uninterested in the food. I decided that Joe might be nice to look at, all bright red hair and blue eyes, but he was boring. He talked about himself an awful lot and what made me really mad was that Claire hung on his every word. She was funny and smart and lovely but at dinner she turned into an airhead. More like the women that Jonathan used to date. She agreed with everything he said. Even when he said he liked hunting, and I knew that Claire hated it. She had told me when I moved in that I should never bring her anything dead, because she didn't believe anything should die just for the sake of it. Had I been able to answer her, I would have said that it was just a cat's way of showing love and affection, but instead I respected her wishes. Now this idiot sat opposite her, talking about shooting seasons and plucking pheasants and she didn't even tell him what she'd told me. I had half a mind to bring her a dead bird to teach her a lesson.

Instead I sulked under the table, unnoticed, until they got up and went back to the sofa. They started kissing in an alarming way, as if they were wrestling with each other. I didn't know whether to go in and save Claire or not, but she didn't sound as if she needed help.

'You're gorgeous,' Joe said, when he took his lips off her for a minute.

'So are you. Come on, let's go to bed.' They both practically ran upstairs without a backward glance; it seemed that they had both forgotten all about me.

Sitting watching the night sky, I was feeling increasingly insecure. I was worried that I was disposable to both Jonathan and Claire, and I really hoped I wasn't. Even with four families, life still felt precarious. Especially now it seemed that both Claire and Jonathan had found 'friends' who didn't like me. This was a turn of events that I hadn't anticipated.

It was one thing to win round owners and other cats, but

these two were something else. Even with Agnes, who was incredibly cold towards me at first, I could see goodness in her. The same was true of Jonathan; although his was well buried, I knew it was there. However I didn't sense any good in either Philippa or Joe, and I was terrified that they would hurt me.

# Chapter
# Twenty-
# Four

It was a rare sight. Franceska was crying. It was a day that Thomasz didn't have to go to work and he had taken both the boys out, telling his wife to have some time to herself and 'put her feet up'. She didn't do this, though. She took out her computer and she made some very thick coffee before speaking to someone on the screen, who I guessed was her mother. She looked similar to her, only with very grey hair and more lines on her face. I sat on her lap at one point and they both laughed. I heard Franceska say my name, so I guessed I was being introduced.

They spoke in Polish for a long time and afterwards Franceska burst into tears. I moved as swiftly as I could to be near her, having long since left her lap, and she scooped me up and held me close. I felt such warmth from this lady, more than any of the other people on the street, although I wasn't usually prone to favouritism.

'Oh, Alfie,' she said, sobbing in a way that made my heart want to break. 'I miss my mamma so much. All my family. Pappa, my sisters, sometimes I think I never see them again.' I looked at her, trying to convey that I did understand. Which I did. My whole being carried such loss with me everywhere I went; I carried it in my fur, my paws and my heart.

'I love my Thomasz and my boys. I know we here for better lives and Thomasz loves his job. He is brilliant chef and here is opportunity. And I know he ambitions when we marry. I know he want his own restaurant and I really think that he get it one day. I must support him. And I do, but I am so lonely and afraid.' I knew how she felt.

'I keep so fine when the boys are around but then when I am alone I feel it all. I no want Thomasz to know because he works so hard and is so tired trying to keep everything in order. Is better job here but is expensive so he worries too. We all worry and sometimes I wonder if it's worth it. Why not stay at home? But also I understand he want more. For him, for us and for the boys.' And my Franceska, my lovely, gorgeous friend, put her head in her hands and sobbed.

We stayed like that for what seemed like a long time. At last she gently put me down, stood up and went to the bathroom. She washed her face and put some stuff on it like Claire does. She straightened up and practised smiling in the mirror.

'I must stop this,' she said, and I wondered if it happened often. I really hoped not. I had never really been alone with her like this before. I had always seen the faraway look in her eyes, but that was only when she snatched moments to herself.

The doorbell rang just as she had recovered herself. She walked down the carpeted stairs in her bare feet. Polly stood on the other side of the door, smiling and holding a bottle of wine.

'Hello!' Franceska looked surprised, as did I; Polly rarely smiled, and this was a more relaxed smile than I had ever seen before.

'Guess what? We just met Matt after work and on the way home, we ran into Thomasz, your Thomasz.' She was breathless with excitement and she looked more beautiful than ever, if that was possible. 'Anyway, the men started talking and they both got onto the subject of football and Matt wanted to show Thomasz some game on the oversized TV – Matt's pride and joy. Not only that, but they promised to feed the children. Which means we can have an hour to ourselves with some wine! Voilà.' Franceska looked confused, then she smiled.

'You better come in before they changes their mind.' They both laughed.

'I know I never normally let Henry out of my sight but he's been taking his solids so well and I've expressed some milk, so, as Matt pointed out, there was no reason at all why I shouldn't have some time to myself. Not to mention a glass of wine.'

Polly followed Franceska into the kitchen, where she poured them both a drink.

'*Na zdrowie*,' Franceska said, holding her glass in the air.

'I'm hoping that that means "cheers",' Polly replied.

They both sat in the living room and I joined them. I tried not to be affronted that Polly hadn't really acknowledged me, but then she rarely did. She seemed to see me as an afterthought, but with her it wasn't that she didn't like me, it was more that she didn't like anything or anyone right now. I knew deep down that she wasn't mean, like the more recent newcomers in my life.

'So, are you OK?' Franceska asked.

'I think so. I know it sounds awful but I haven't been away from Henry since he was born. Not even for an hour. I mean I've been asleep while Matt looked after him, but never in a different house. This is the furthest I've been.'

'Sometimes we mothers need breaks.'

'Yes, we do. But then I already feel guilty.' It seemed Polly's earlier joy was short lived as her eyes clouded.

'Mother's guilt, it come as soon as you get pregnant.' Franceska laughed weakly.

'I guess so, that's what Mum said. I miss my mum.' Polly's eyes flecked with sadness.

'Oh so do I. I miss so much.'

'You see, we have a lot in common,' Polly smiled. Her teeth were so white and perfect. I was sure this woman could have been a model.

'In this case, we must get used to taking the gifts when our husbands give. Mine is too busy to do this much.'

'Mine too. Right, and no more moaning, we will enjoy ourselves. It's just an hour and I think it's important that we make the most of it.'

'Good. You know, Polly, you are my first English friend.'

'And you're my first London friend. And the only Polish friend I have, actually. I'm so glad you live next door.' The two women were getting sentimental and I felt a bit emotional too. It had been that sort of day all round.

By the time Polly left, they had only had a couple of drinks, but they were both giggling and happy. Thomasz came home with the boys and Polly went, looking as good as when she'd arrived.

'Bye, Frankie,' she said, kissing her cheek and using the more affectionate version of her name, which Franceska said she preferred. 'Matt, he is nice man,' Thomasz said, when they were alone.

'Nice family. I think we can be friends.'

'Yes, I am thinking they look down on us because we are Polish.' Thomasz's face darkened.

'I know, but not everyone is like that. We are lucky our neighbours aren't.' Franceska's eyes clouded over.

'But others ...'

'Let's not talk about it, Thomasz. I really don't want to.' Her face was taut with worry.

'Sorry, but I think we should.'

'It is one woman and she will soon stop. Old lady, she no understand modern world.'

'But we don't take benefits and I won't have you upset in the street.'

'Please, leave it, Thomasz, you hardly ever have day off. Please don't ruin.' She left the room to go to the boys and I wondered what she meant and what I was missing? It sounded like someone had said something bad to her. If I ever found out who, I would go and hiss, spit and scratch them for making my Franceska sad.

As I sat at the front door to be let out I had more questions than answers, but it was time to check on Claire and Jonathan. It was also time for me to go and see what was being served for dinner.

# Chapter
# Twenty-
# Five

It was getting worse. I was becoming a very worried cat. My plan so far had not been without hiccups but I did think it had, on the whole, been working brilliantly. But over the past month, it had all started going wrong.

Jonathan was staying out more and more, usually forgetting to leave me any food. Then, when I next saw him, he would be all contrite, although he would smile like a lunatic cat, so I didn't believe him at all. He was suddenly very happy with the dreadful Philippa. And she wasn't very happy with me. Every time she came to our house, she would make a big fuss about me being allowed on the furniture and about how unhygienic I was; a blatant lie, as I was one of the cleanest cats I knew. I took great pride in my appearance; but she just didn't like me. Yesterday evening, I arrived at Jonathan's at dinner time. The woman, Philippa, was sat on the sofa, my sofa, next to Jonathan. He was reading a big paper, she was reading a magazine, and they were sitting there as if they had been together for a long time. It made me bristle with annoyance. Jonathan looked up.

'Alfie, I was wondering where you were. I left some food out for you in the kitchen.' I looked at him; I hadn't walked past any food.

'Oh no, I put it in the fridge, it's disgusting to leave food out,' Philippa said. I gave her my meanest look, and even Jonathan raised his eyebrows. He got up and walked to the kitchen. I followed him. He found my food in the fridge and put it down for me.

'Sorry, mate,' he said, as he went back to the living room.

They were still sitting in the same place after I'd eaten. I jumped onto Jonathan's lap to thank him for the food.

'You don't mind that?' Philippa asked, looking at him disapprovingly. She had a bit of a snooty face if you asked me.

'No, not at all. He's a good cat.'

'I don't think it's sensible to encourage pets on the furniture.'

'He's fine, he doesn't shed much hair.' It was funny hearing Jonathan defend me. After all, when we'd first met, he'd accused me of all sorts and he didn't like me on his furniture, or even in his house at all.

'Well, it just doesn't seem like a good idea. What does he do when you're at work? Where did he sleep last night?' I wanted to scratch her again. She was so rude!

'He does what cats do. He hunts, hangs out with other cats. He seems quite happy and he always comes home at some point, so why worry?'

'It just isn't practical for people like us to have pets,' she said. 'And if you're happy not knowing where he is …'

'Why do I feel we are talking about a teenager rather than a cat?' He laughed. She smiled, tightly. It made her look as though her face would split.

'Anyway, Jon, can you drive me home? As much as I'd like to stay and talk about the cat, I need to go and prepare for work tomorrow.'

'Of course, hon. I'll get my keys. But I'll have to come straight back, I have some figures to go over.'

When Jonathan left to get his keys, she looked at me really nastily. I hissed at her and she laughed.

'Don't think you are any match for me,' she snarled, before turning on the charm when Jonathan returned.

Saddest of all, when they went to bed, there would be no cashmere blanket for me. I followed them into the room once and Philippa shrieked like I was about to kill her. If only I could! Jonathan picked me up, took me to the landing and closed the bedroom door, shutting me out. He only wanted me when she wasn't there, it seemed.

And although Jonathan would swat away her criticism of me, I felt as if he didn't really fight my cause, which was disappointing. For a while I was his only friend and now he seemed to have forgotten that. What a Judas!

Claire was no better. My lovely, sweet Claire was so smitten with Joe that she seemed to think he was the master of the universe. When he said anything, she would agree with him, or laugh as if he was funny, when he really wasn't. The problem with this relationship was that Joe always came to her house. He said his flat wasn't very big and he had an annoying flatmate, so he had been staying at Claire's loads since their first dinner. It was as if he had practically moved in. And although he didn't say anything bad about me to Claire, he was worse than Philippa, because he pretended he liked me and then when she wasn't there, he would look at me as if I was the worst thing ever. Once, he had literally tried to kick me out of the way. It was only thanks to my speedy reactions that I was able to dodge him. Of course this seemed to make him even angrier, but he never showed it around Claire. And although Claire always made sure I was fed, she pretty much ignored me when Joe was around; I wasn't welcome any more. I knew when I wasn't wanted.

My Margaret had been so reliable, but these people weren't. I asked Tiger about it but she said that she didn't know.

Her owners didn't ever go away without looking out for her and they weren't mean. But then, they were both cat lovers. I wished that Jonathan and Claire were with cat lovers. I knew that if my future was going to be secure I needed Joe and Philippa out of my life and therefore out of Claire and Jonathan's. I just wasn't sure yet how on earth I was going to achieve that.

The other problem I had was the weather. I had always been a fair weather cat until forced into homelessness. Then I had braved all elements and survived, but of course I hated it. The rain hadn't stopped all week. Claire said it was because we'd had an early summer, but I didn't understand how that could cause rain. The rain was pretty much continuous, the showers were heavy and I had only managed to brave the walk to number 22 once, so it had been a few days since I'd seen Franceska, Polly and the others. I sat on either Claire or Jonathan's windowsills, watching the rain splatter the windows with a heavy heart.

I was at Claire's, looking out of the window, when Joe and Claire came downstairs.

'Sorry darling, but I'll feed Alfie and then I have to run, I have an early meeting.'

'No time for coffee with me?' he asked.

'It's because of you I'm running late,' she giggled. 'If you want coffee, do you mind letting yourself out?'

'Not at all,' he said, pinching her bottom and grinning. I couldn't believe my eyes as she went to the kitchen to feed me, then went to put a coat on, before leaving the house. He watched her go and then he looked at me.

'You don't want to be out in that rain, do you?' he said. I miaowed, uncertainly. 'Well tough.' He picked me up roughly by the neck and threw me out of the front door. I landed on my feet, but I was upset, sore from where he had grabbed me, and I was getting wet. Shaking myself off in anger, I stalked away.

I reasoned that since I was already wet I would brave it and try to go and see the others at the number 22 flats. When I got there, my fur was soaked right through. I miaowed and scratched on Franceska's door but there was no answer. I couldn't hear anything from Polly's flat either, so I wondered if they had all gone out together, although the weather was so bad I didn't know why on earth they would. I felt so dejected. As the rain started to ease off, I wandered down to the pond in the park. It had been such an awful morning so far, that I decided to cheer myself up by going to find a butterfly or a bird to chase. It didn't occur to me that they would all be sheltering from the rain. I got to the pond and found it deserted. So instead, I contented myself with trying to chase my reflection. I got as close as I could but the grass was muddy and before I knew it, I started to slide. I desperately tried to use my claws to grip on to the pond bank, but it was useless; it was so slippery that despite scrabbling to get away from the dark water below, I only slid ever closer to the freezing depths. I yowled loudly, terrified, not knowing what I would do if I fell into the cold water – I couldn't swim and I had no idea how to get out. Again, I desperately tried to find the bank as I saw yet another of my nine lives flash before me. I used my paws to try to find something, anything, I could cling on to. I cried out as loudly as I could, but I felt hope deserting me as I realised I couldn't hold on any longer and pitched tail-first into the pond. I heard a loud 'splash' as I hit the water. The first thing I noticed was the cold as I was submerged. I screeched again as

I tried to pull myself out of the water but my head kept being submerged. I felt as if I was losing any strength I had to stop myself from drowning.

'Alfie, is that you?' I heard a familiar voice shout; as my head briefly reached the surface I saw it was Matt. I tried to cry out again but no sound came. All I could hear was the whooshing of the water as my head bobbed up and down.

'Alfie, try to swim, I'll get you.' Matt was shouting. I used my paws to try to paddle for my life, and I glimpsed Matt, on his knees in the mud, trying to lean forward.

'I've got a stick, try to grab it,' he said as I briefly saw him waving a branch at me. I tried to grab it with my paws but it was too far away and I went under the water again. The next time I came to the surface I saw Matt was practically in the pond with me.

'Alfie, nearly there. Please try to keep still.' I heard the pleading in his voice and I felt his arm try to grab me but the water pulled me under again.

I had no energy left and I felt as if I couldn't fight any more but I tried desperately to reach the surface yet again. My eyes were closed as I felt an arm grab at me. I screeched as I felt the grip tighten and then suddenly all was still. I opened my eyes to find myself lying on the bank of the pond on top of Matt who was soaked from the rain and his clothes covered in mud.

'Oh God, I thought you were a goner,' he said, as he clutched me to him. I was so exhausted I couldn't say anything; I just collapsed into his arms. 'Let's get you home and dry and then I'll see if you need a vet.' I was so weak with relief that I didn't move.

When we got into the flat, he took me through to the bathroom and wrapped me in a fluffy towel. He then went and changed into clean clothes. I snuggled into the towel, still too exhausted to move. He carried me gently into the living room and put me on the sofa. He brought me some milk in a bowl and I drank it gratefully.

'What were you doing, falling in a pond?' he asked. I yelped. 'Well, I guess you'll stay away when it's this wet and muddy. You poor little thing. Are you OK now?' I purred. I felt my strength returning and Matt was making me feel better. I was cross with myself for taking risks, but at least I had seven lives still intact.

'Are you wondering where they are? Polly, Franceska and the kids?' he asked. I miaowed, quietly. 'They've gone away. Franceska took the boys to Poland, for a few weeks. Thomasz booked it as a surprise. Then Polly got a virus, so we decided it was best she go to her mum's until she's better. I'm going to spend the weekends there until she's ready to come back.' He stroked my drying fur. 'I'm supposed to be working from home this afternoon so you can hang out with me!' He was so cheerful and kind, I fleetingly felt better.

I felt so grateful to Matt, although sad that Franceska and Aleksy weren't there in my hour of need after my near death experience. I knew I was feeling sorry for myself, mainly because of the horrible Joe, but Matt's kindness had made me feel better. I did sense some of my loneliness returning; I missed my families.

Obviously, because I hadn't visited recently due to the weather, they hadn't been able to tell me that they were going away. I knew from the last time I had seen Franceska that she needed her mamma, plus Polly needed something too. So I tried to be less selfish and feel glad that although they were gone, they would be back. It was only going to be a few weeks, which wasn't too long. Not even for an insecure cat like me.

After drinking my milk, I curled up and slept on Matt and Polly's sofa and I dreamt of everyone that I loved – from my past, Margaret and Agnes, and from my present, Claire, Jonathan, Franceska, the boys and Polly, Matt and Henry. Just because things weren't perfect, I had no cause to complain. It wasn't so long ago that I'd had no one, so I needed to be more grateful for where I was now.

I woke up hours later and felt better and drier. I shook myself and got off the sofa, leaving the towel, wet from my damp fur. I jumped onto Matt's lap to get his attention and then I went and stood by the front door.

'Ah, you want to go?' He smiled. 'At least that means you are OK now. It's funny, we all wonder where you go when you leave here, but I guess you have a home that's expecting you.' I cocked my head to one side. Matt opened the door. 'Bye Alfie, visit any time.'

I waited at Claire's for her to come home from work. Still a little bit shaken by the events of the morning, I curled up in my bed and tried to get warm. Although I was dry, the cold-ness you get from being wet through had lingered and I was still a little traumatised.

I heard Claire's key in the door and she walked in. She was alone so I went up to her and made a massive fuss. I needed her love. I really did, more than ever. She rewarded me with a loving cuddle before she put me down and went to feed me.

'You seem a bit soppy today,' she said, as she put my food on the mat. I was practically stuck to her legs. 'Not that I'm com-plaining,' she laughed. 'I feel as though you've been cross with me lately. Tash said it might be because you're jealous of all the attention I've been giving to Joe.'

I wanted to tell her that Tasha was wrong, I wasn't jealous, I was bloody annoyed. But of course I could only miaow and I wasn't sure how much that conveyed.

'Ah, Alfie, you're still my main man.' She tickled me affectionately. 'But I'll make more of an effort to ensure that you know that.' She laughed again and I wanted to tell her that it was no joking matter.

Her phone rang as I was eating.

'Oh, hi, Tasha, thanks for calling me back,' she said cheerily. There was a pause. 'No, sorry, I was going to come to book club but Joe called on my way home and he's had a really bad day at work. I said he could come round so I can't come tonight.' There was another pause. 'No, of course I'm not putting him before friends, but he sounded so dejected. Apparently a client has complained about him. It's awful.' Another pause. 'Oh thanks for being so understanding, let's have a drink tomorrow night, I promise I won't cancel on you.'

I was angry with Tasha then; why was she understanding? Why did Claire have to put this awful man before all of us? I blamed him for my near drowning experience, after all he'd thrown me out that morning.

By the time Joe arrived, Claire had changed her clothes, put on more make-up and tidied the already spotless house.

'Hello, you,' she said, giving him a warm hug.

'Have you got any beer?' he asked, without returning the hug or even saying hello.

'Yes, I got some in for you, I'll get you one.' She looked puzzled and hurt. I heard warning bells again. He wasn't as nice to her as he had been when he first started coming round.

Not only did he not like me, but now he was acting as if he didn't like her either. This wasn't the sort of man I wanted for my Claire. I felt suddenly fearful that this was about more than my fragile ego. He sat himself down on the sofa and flicked the TV on with the remote control. Claire brought him his drink and sat next to him.

'So, do you want to talk about it?' she asked, tentatively.

'Actually I want to watch the football. It's about to start. Have you made dinner?'

'No, I was going to book club before you called, so I don't have anything in.'

'OK, well why don't you order us a Chinese?'

'Oh, OK. What do you want?' She sounded hurt by his coldness and I felt hurt for her. He hadn't said please or thank you or anything.

'Spare ribs, sweet and sour pork and egg fried rice.' He went back to watching the TV screen and Claire left the room. I followed her as she went into the kitchen and opened a drawer to take out a takeaway menu. I rubbed her legs.

'He's only like this because he's worried about work,' she whispered, and I made a hissing sound in response. He was like this because he was horrible. I was being proved right. I had known that he was rotten when I first met him. I had a cat's instinct about him and that was never wrong.

Everything was a pretence with him; pretending to like me and pretending to be nice to Claire. Now he was shedding his niceness. It seemed Claire was not good at choosing men, although she had struck lucky with me of course. But then Claire didn't know my main rule in life; never trust a person who doesn't like cats.

I wanted to see Jonathan but I didn't want to leave Claire

in such a vulnerable position. I had a feeling she would need me more than ever. I could see she was shaken and confused as she waited for the takeaway, sitting next to Joe in silence. When it arrived, he didn't move or offer to pay, leaving her to pay for it and dish it out onto plates.

'Are you going to come and eat?' she asked, as she put everything on the table.

'I'm watching the match, can't I eat it here?' he snapped.

She looked at him with very sad eyes.

'I really don't like eating on the sofa,' she said, again, sounding timid. 'You can see the TV from here.'

'Oh, for God's sake,' he shouted, aggressively. Claire jumped. I stretched myself up as tall as I could and hissed at him.

'Don't you hiss at me,' he said, standing up. Claire looked lost but I wasn't scared. I spat at him and hissed again.

'You flea-ridden, mangy ball of fur,' he shouted, looking as if he fancied killing me. I recoiled into a ball, and yowled in fear.

'Joe, what the hell do you think you're doing, shouting at Alfie like that?' Claire said. Her voice was quiet, but strong. Joe looked at her. I could see he was working out his next move.

'Sorry,' he said, as if he didn't really mean it. 'Sorry, I shouldn't have. Sorry, Alfie. I'd never hurt him you know. It's just work, it's hell. Oh Claire, I'm sorry. Let's go and eat dinner. I'll make it up to you, I promise.'

She looked unsure but she followed him and they sat down together. He reached over and took her hand.

'I'm so sorry, really I am, darling,' he said. I could practically see his insincerity.

'It's OK. But will you talk to me? What happened at work?'

'This client of mine made a big mistake on his account. He

got the budget for his campaign totally wrong, so when we went to bill them, he went mad, and then to cover his tracks he's trying to blame me.'

'That's awful,' Claire said.

'The problem is that it's a good client and they're threatening to take their business away. So I have to be the fall guy in the eyes of the agency. They've suspended me, pending an investigation, blah, blah, blah.'

'But the truth will come out?' Claire looked so worried.

'Of course, it'll be fine, it's just politics, but in the meantime I've been told not to come back for the next week. I mean, how humiliating!'

'I do understand, hon, and you know I'll support you.'

'I really am sorry and I do appreciate you, you know.' Joe smiled. His charming façade was back on his face and Claire lapped it up as if he was a saucer of cream.

I wanted to scream at her, trying to make her understand that he was full of rubbish. I could imagine the support he would want; lots more free Chinese takeaways, lots of watching football whilst being handed beers; I had heard about this kind of man before.

My cat instincts told me that Joe was the cause of the problem at work. It was definitely his fault and more than ever, I realised that he wasn't good enough, no way near good enough, for my Claire.

# Chapter
# Twenty-Six

I was at Jonathan's, waiting for him to come home from work and fervently hoping he would arrive soon.

Another week had passed and things were deteriorating further. When I had set my cat heart on Edgar Road, I had felt as if all my troubles were over. The excitement of finding homes and people had long since passed. There was too much worry, too much uncertainty, but by now I was too emotionally invested into their lives to just leave. Not that I had anywhere to go, of course.

I missed the families at number 22. There wasn't much point visiting, as they were still away, although I couldn't help myself walking down there sometimes and pining for my friends.

Going to Jonathan's wasn't too bad. Despite the fact that the horrible Philippa was there quite a lot, it didn't matter too much. At least I knew where I was with her, and although she wasn't nice to me, she was nice to Jonathan. Well, she was sometimes but she seemed to always tell him what to do, not that he seemed to mind. The more I tried to understand these humans, the less I understood them.

That night, Jonathan came home and made a huge fuss of me, which took me by surprise.

'Philippa's gone away on business, so it's just you and me for the next few days.' I licked my lips in delight. I shouldn't have been so happy; after all, Jonathan only wanted me because his stupid girlfriend had gone away, but I was grateful for any affection and love he showed me. I decided to make the most of our time together; if Jonathan remembered how charming I was, he might never let Philippa criticise me or call me names again.

Despite the fact that I had to check on Claire regularly (and the increasingly lazy Joe), Jonathan and I had a lovely boys' time together. We definitely re-bonded with touch and smell, and I gave him a couple of little gifts to show that he was back in my good books.

The strange thing was that, although he spoke to Philippa at night, I got the feeling that he was happier without her. It was weird, but when she was there, he seemed to have to be on his guard all the time. He was polite and tidy and cleaned up. But without her, he wore his gym clothes, he left plates on the side overnight, and he was so much more relaxed. I'm not sure the mess was a good thing, by the way, never having been a slovenly cat myself. But nevertheless, I wondered why humans were so stupid. Claire had been happier without Joe, I was pretty sure, and Jonathan was happier without Philippa. When Claire had come back from seeing her mum, she had thrown herself into her friendship with Tasha and the book club and seemed quite happy. Now, with Joe, there was something missing again. Her sparkle had gone. And Jonathan seemed tense when Philippa was around, and he actually seemed pleased she had gone away.

I really didn't understand them at all. Not one bit.

Over the next few days, Jonathan and I developed a little routine. I still made sure that I spent enough time with Claire, but I spent even more with Jonathan. We ate together, and yes, I had so much fresh fish, I was in heaven. I didn't even miss my sardines. We watched TV together. He would slump on the sofa with his beer and I would sit nestled into his side while he would absently stroke me. We went up to bed together again and the cashmere blanket returned. He talked to me, as well: about work, which he was enjoying; his new friends, who he was planning on drinking with at the weekend; and his gym, which he went to often, as he didn't want to 'let himself go', The only thing he didn't talk to me about was Philippa, which said it all really.

But still, every evening when they spoke on the phone he would end the call by telling her that he missed her. He even said he loved her. I couldn't believe it; I just didn't believe he really did.

It was at this point that I developed another plan. Everything that had happened had changed me and given me new ideas. It seemed clear to me what I needed to do. Jonathan couldn't really be happy with Philippa, and Joe wasn't good enough for my Claire, so I had the brilliant idea of getting Claire and Jonathan together. After all, I had been the one who started the friendship between Franceska and Polly! Claire and Jonathan both loved me and I knew they would be perfect together. I just needed to try to figure out a way to make it happen.

One day, I tried hard to get Jonathan to follow me out of the house by miaowing very loudly as if something was wrong, when I knew Claire would be nearby, but his mobile phone rang and by the time he came off the call, it was too late to engineer the meeting. Another time, I tried to get Claire to follow me to Jonathan's by yelping and then running off. But she thought I was playing and told me not to be such a 'silly cat'. So far, I had no more ideas on how to get them together, but I was a determined cat and I knew I wouldn't give up.

I couldn't give up. I was seriously worried about Claire. Joe hadn't left Claire's house since the night of the Chinese. Well he had, but only to get a bag of his stuff and come back. He sat around all day watching TV and eating her food, and then, when she came home in the evening, he would be mean to her and then apologise, blaming the stress of his job situation. He had tried to kick me a number of times and although I managed to dodge him, he was becoming more menacing each time. I couldn't leave, because I was worried about Claire, but I was getting increasingly anxious when I was actually there.

There was no sign of Tasha, and I missed her. There was just Joe, sitting on Claire's sofa, with no intention of moving, and Claire, running around him like a timid mouse.

The way he was treating her, I knew I had to get Joe out of our lives. But it was as if he had cast a spell on her. She didn't seem happy any more, but I don't think she realised it, as she spent more and more time trying to please Joe. It was another human contradiction I couldn't understand. I wished I could talk to Tasha, because I was sure that between us we would sort something out. I was certain that she would have noticed what had happened to her friend, but of course I couldn't do that. So instead I became a bit of an invisible, stealth cat. I became adept at keeping out of his way, hiding behind furniture, but with my ears pricked up so I could hear everything. I knew that he spoke on the phone a lot when she was out. I knew he wasn't really ever going to get his job back because I had been right all along – it was his fault. I was pretty sure that he had no intention of leaving Claire's house, because he was giving up his flat. This was turning into a terrible mess.

When Claire was home, I would make myself seen. She was still fussing me and feeding me but I could see the way Joe was beginning to affect her. She looked tired and worried all day, and she was definitely getting thin again.

That evening, she got home from work and the first thing Joe asked was what they were having for dinner.

'I've got steak,' she answered, sounding weary.

'OK, good. Let me know when it's ready.' When Claire was home, he watched TV all the time, drank beer and let Claire do everything. He didn't tidy the house or clean, he didn't shop or even cook. And she never said anything to him, although I knew this must upset her, being such a tidy person herself. Even I knew not to leave my cat toys lying around.

I was pretty sure that he would never leave, and the worst thing was that I didn't think Claire would ask him to leave, either. I realised I couldn't abandon Claire to this horrible man that I didn't trust – it made my job on this street even more important. It was in the darkest times that I would be needed the most.

I wondered, almost on a daily basis, how I had got to this. I'd gone from a loving, largely simple home with Margaret and Agnes, to having to fight for survival, living in two main homes and two part-time ones. Now I was in a complete tailspin about everyone. I was only a cat, for goodness sake. I wasn't built to deal with so much turmoil.

# Chapter Twenty-Seven

Chapter
Twenty
Seven

Thank goodness; finally, it was a day of homecomings. On my walk to number 22, I saw Polly through the window of her flat. She was holding Henry and he seemed to be asleep. I also saw that Franceska and the boys were with her. I jumped onto the windowsill, and I heard Aleksy shout, 'Alfie,' in glee. Franceska said something to Polly and then she came to the door and let me in.

Ah, what a welcome. Aleksy was all over me, as was Thomasz, who seemed bigger than when he had left. Franceska smiled so much and even Polly seemed a tiny bit pleased to see me. She also looked much happier and healthier; her eyes didn't have their usual dark rings.

'I miss you, I miss you,' Aleksy kept saying, over and over. It was so lovely and if I had been able to cry, it would have brought a happy tear to my eye. Instead, I had a massive cat grin stuck to my face for the rest of the afternoon.

'How do you feel about being back here?' Polly asked Franceska, as she put Henry into his cot and went to make a drink for them both.

'I am OK. It was so nice to go home, see my family, so good. But I miss Thomasz, the boys miss him and I see that our home is here now. I sad to leave but happy to come back. Does it make sense?'

'Yes. And I'm so pleased to see you, but I didn't want to come back. I mean, of course I missed Matt, but having my mum help with Henry was just so nice. Even when I started to feel better I preferred being there to here, which sounds so terrible. I know

I need to be more like you about living in London, but I really dreaded coming back.' She looked sad again.

'Oh Polly, I sorry. But you must speak with Matt about it.'

'There's no point. His career is so important. I mean, I was a model, and there's no way I can go back to that now that I've had Henry, not that I want to. So we have to do what's best for our future and it's here; Matt's job is here. Not only does he earn so much more than he did in Manchester, but also there are far more opportunities. I just wish I was better at this mum stuff.'

'Oh Polly, you fine. It's hard, that's all. I never found it easy and only now the boys are bigger it gets better. But maybe your mum comes here?'

'Have you seen the size of this flat? Of course you have, it's the same size as yours!' She laughed, which was a good sign.

'No room, I know. Anyways, we make the best of things, yes?'

'Yes, Frankie, we will. And you are so good at that, you know.'

'I struggle. Polly, I didn't tell you, before we went away, why we went ... Thomasz made me go. Someone on the street was very bad to me. They hear me talk to Aleksy, in Polish, I forgot, and they say, "Foreigners only come here for our money and free living, you should go home."'

'That's awful.' Now I knew what she had been talking about before she went away and what she was crying about. My poor Franceska.

'Yes but it not young boy or what you call it?'

'Yob?'

'No, it old lady. With the grey hair. She say it every time I see her. And we no have nothing free.'

'I know you don't. Honestly, don't listen to people like that. There might always be prejudice, but it's just narrow-mindedness.'

'It hurts that people might say it to my children.'

'Look, when Aleksy starts school at the end of the summer he'll be fine. He'll make loads of friends and you'll see that it's not as bad as you think.' It was funny hearing Polly being reassuring and positive – it was usually the other way around.

'Thank you. Meeting you makes me feel hopeful, that people will be like you. Not like that old lady.'

'You're normally the one reassuring me!' Polly said, again reading my mind, and went over to Franceska and gave her a hug. My cat heart felt warm. I felt as if I was instrumental in this beautiful friendship that had sprung up between them, and it was one good thing that I had managed to do. I was fearful that I was losing my Claire and that Jonathan wouldn't be so close to me when Philippa came back, so I would hold on to this tightly. It would make me smile when I was feeling sad.

When Franceska went back to her flat to make tea for the boys, I left Polly's and wandered back to Claire's house. But she wasn't there. I felt excited that she might have gone out after work for once, and when I saw Joe lying on the sofa, I made a swift exit. I went to Jonathan's and let myself in the cat flap. Then I started as I saw Philippa, sat at the kitchen table in front of a computer. She was wearing a dress, which she never normally did. She looked as if she had made a big effort and I fleetingly wondered how she had got in, as Jonathan clearly wasn't here. I miaowed, loudly.

'Oh, you bloody cat,' she exclaimed, jumping slightly. 'I was hoping that my homecoming would be cat free. Shoo.'

What did she mean, 'homecoming'? This wasn't her home.

I began to panic. What if, like Joe, she had moved in? I ran into the living room and sulked under a chair waiting for Jonathan.

'Hello?' he shouted, as he opened the front door.

'In the kitchen,' Philippa replied. He went through and I followed him. She jumped up and threw her arms around his neck, kissing him. She looked as if she was sucking the very life out of him. I rubbed against his leg, trying to remind him that this week I'd been his best friend.

'My two favourite people. Well, person and cat,' he joshed, as he bent down to stroke me.

'Can you leave the cat alone and concentrate on me? In fact, let's go upstairs – we have time to make up.'

'Let me just feed him first,' Jonathan said, which pleased me, but Philippa's face looked like thunder. He put some prawns in a bowl for me and then they went upstairs. I knew when I was beaten, but at least I got prawns out of it.

Much later, they emerged. She was wearing one of Jonathan's T-shirts and he was wearing a robe.

'What do you fancy eating?' he asked.

'Apart from you?' she said, giggling. She was acting very strangely. Maybe, like Claire, she had drunk too much wine, although I hadn't seen any pass her lips.

'Why don't you order a curry? I know it's your favourite,' she said. 'And we can open the champagne I brought.'

'Sounds good to me.' They spent time discussing what they would eat and then Jonathan ordered the food, opened the champagne and poured it into thin, posh looking glasses.

'Let's raise a toast,' Philippa said.

'To what?' Jonathan asked.

'To us and the fact that I think we should move in together.'

I was glad I didn't have a drink, otherwise I would have choked on it.

'Really? Move in together?' Jonathan said. I was gratified to see that he looked a little bit shocked too. 'But we haven't been together that long!'

'I know, but we've known each other for years and anyway, why not? I mean we clearly get on well and, you know, at our age I don't see the point of waiting.'

'It's just a bit sudden, and, well, totally out of the blue. Isn't this something we should discuss together?' I wasn't sure if Jonathan looked confused or terrified. I was definitely terrified, however. I felt my luck was really on a downward spiral.

'Oh, don't be a typical man. Look, I was away, I missed you. Since we started seeing each other we've been together all the time. This is a logical step.'

'But …'

'I know, we've only been dating for a couple of months, but when you know, you know! Johnny, you're forty-three and I'm about to turn forty. We are both successful, attractive, intelligent people. What's the point in waiting?' I kind of had to give her credit for her confidence; she certainly seemed to know what she wanted.

'Well, I'm not sure.' I noticed that Jonathan hadn't touched his bubbly drink. I think he looked as if he was turning a bit green, actually.

'About me?' Philippa snapped.

'Of course not. I'm sure about you, just not about this. I mean, where would we live?' He looked relieved as he asked the question.

'Well, not here, of course. I mean the house is nice enough, but the postcode isn't great. My apartment in Kensington would suit us both perfectly.'

'I know yours is a nice place and a great location, but I really like it here.' He looked a bit hurt at the criticism of our house. I wondered how Jonathan, who had seemed so arrogant and confident when I first met him, would even entertain the idea of being with such a woman. I know she wasn't bad to look at but really, her personality wasn't at all good enough.

'It's fine, but you know it's just a bit further out of town than is convenient. Also, you could rent this place out to a family, it'd make a good rental.'

'I've only just moved in though, really.'

'Jonathan, what is wrong with you? I am offering you myself, full time, in my gorgeous Kensington apartment. Imagine, we can entertain in style, which will be good for our careers. I mean this isn't great to invite people to – it's not really in the best area, is it?'

'All right, Philippa,' Jonathan snapped. 'I get it. I'm just not sure that I want to move in to your place.'

'Don't be silly, of course you do.' I marvelled that her confidence hadn't slipped one bit.

'I really like you, and we've been having a great time together, but can't we just leave things as they are? Just for the time being.' He seemed to be begging a bit. I was beginning to feel happy inside. So far, Jonathan had seemed to really like this woman, and although he wasn't like Claire was with Joe, which was timid and scared, I honestly thought she did exert a lot of control over him.

'No, Jonathan, we can't. I want to settle down. I'm thirty-nine. I want to be a partner in the firm this year and they favour married people, or at least settled ones. I want to get married. I want a child before I turn forty-one. There is no waiting to be done.'

'Woah Phil, slow down. Where is this coming from?' I retreated a bit, and it seemed Jonathan was physically recoiling from her too. 'As you said, we've only been seeing each other for a couple of months. Before you went away on business we were having a lovely time. Going to dinner, spending time here, everything was great but not that serious. You can't come back from a business trip to New York and demand I move in with you, marry you and impregnate you.' He laughed, uncertainly.

'I can and I have. Look Jonathan, this makes sense. Look at you. You had this high-flying career in Singapore and you've had to take a considerable step back in your work here.'

'Thanks for reminding me.' He looked unhappy, so I went up to him and rubbed his legs under the table.

'My point is that I have a great job and prospects. You can support me and work your way back up at the same time. We will be a great team. I'll make you look good and vice versa.'

'You make it sound like a business relationship,' he said, sounding sad.

'Of course not, but, well, I'm not the queen of romance, you know that. Anyway, that's what I want and what I want, I get.' She did look determined; her eyes steely.

They sat in silence for a few minutes. I suddenly wondered what the logistics of such a move would mean for me. I didn't know where Kensington was, or how far from here. I had a horrible feeling that I wouldn't be able to go and visit him, as it would be too far. I'd have to stay here with the people who rented this house. I loved Jonathan but I also loved Claire, and Franceska's family, and I was growing fond of Polly and Matt. I felt terror creep up my fur. I didn't want him to go, because what if I never saw him again? It hit me that I loved him.

'What about Alfie?' Jonathan asked suddenly. I wanted to

pounce with joy. Philippa looked at him through narrowed eyes.

'Cats aren't allowed in my apartment building,' she said, heartlessly.

'I can't leave him,' Jonathan replied quietly.

'Oh, for God's sake. Cats get re-homed all the time. You can find him a family to go to, we'll do an advert. He's not even your cat in the first place!'

'Philippa, are you completely uncaring? Alfie *is* my cat. I love him.' I felt my fur warm up; he loved me, too. I hissed loudly at Philippa.

'You bloody horrible cat,' she screeched. 'Did you hear how he hissed at me?' She looked thunderous.

'Well, you called him names,' Jonathan replied, seriously.

'Oh, for God's sake, Jonathan. He came with the house, you've barely known him five minutes. It's not great for your image, if I'm honest and let's face it, he's just a bloody cat.'

'I've known him longer than I've been with you,' Jonathan said quietly. 'And when I first came back, I was in a pretty bad way; he sort of saved me.' I felt my heart swell with pride. I saved him! He had noticed, after all.

'He saved you?'

'He was here for me when I felt alone.' Jonathan looked a little bit surprised at this revelation; I basked in the glory of his acknowledgement.

'Right, well, if you're going to be so stupid over a dumb animal, you're not the man I thought you were. I'm going home now, to give you time to come to your senses.'

She got up, looked murderously at Jonathan, and went upstairs to collect her things. We could hear her stomping around and slamming doors angrily, but Jonathan didn't move, and neither did I. I curled myself up against his leg.

She emerged after a while, and stood at the door.

'You'll regret this. What kind of idiot man chooses a cat over me? No wonder you're such a huge failure,' she spat, more viciously than any cat I'd seen.

'Bye, Philippa,' Jonathan said, harshly, and then we watched the door shake as she left, slamming it behind her.

'I didn't see that coming,' Jonathan said, after a while. 'Goodness me. What a woman. I don't know how she went from being a fun casual girlfriend to a psychopath.' I wanted to say that she was never fun to me, but I couldn't. 'Anyway, looks like I've had a lucky escape and Alfie, it looks as if you've saved me yet again.' I purred, proudly. I was so happy and wanted to tell Jonathan that he was very welcome. I had saved us both from the wicked witch. And the bonus was that, although he might have still been in shock a bit, he didn't seem sad. I just hoped that he wouldn't regret it and change his mind. But for now I had to trust him. He had earned my trust after all.

'And the right woman is just around the corner.'

That reminded me of my plan. 'She's not round the corner, she's just down the street,' I wanted to scream. We'd got rid of Philippa, now we just needed to get rid of Joe, and get Claire and Jonathan together. How, I had no idea, but it would make me the happiest cat alive, if I could pull it off. My heart was beating with excitement at the thought that I was a step closer to my ideal goal.

# Chapter Twenty-Eight

I didn't go back to Claire's house that night; I didn't want to leave Jonathan. He'd shown loyalty to me, and I wanted to show mine to him. After Philippa had left, we watched TV together, and then he took me back up to his room and the much-loved cashmere blanket. I had glorious dreams that night, in which I felt loved and warm and wanted. After the last few weeks, where I had felt utter turmoil and insecurity, it was much needed. It was the best cat sleep I'd had in a while.

It wasn't a work day the next day, but I woke early and went and nudged Jonathan by sitting on his chest. He groaned, opened his eyes and gently swatted me away in surprise. I retaliated by softly pawing his nose.

'Ow, Alfie, you startled me,' he groaned. I smiled. I was too happy to be worried about being told off. 'Oh God, I guess you're hungry. OK, come on then. Give me a chance to go for a pee and I'll fetch you some breakfast.' I miaowed joyfully. 'Christ, maybe I should have kept Philippa after all, she's less trouble than you.' I looked at him, shocked but he laughed. 'Only joking. Right, see you downstairs in a minute.' He dashed into his ensuite shower room and I padded downstairs to wait for my breakfast.

We didn't rush but after we had both eaten, Jonathan announced that he was going to the gym and so I thought it was time for me to go and see Claire. I steeled myself for what I might find; who knew what Joe had got up to since I saw them last?

I let myself in and found Claire cooking a big breakfast.

'I was wondering where you were,' she said. 'I was getting worried, Alfie.' She looked so sad as I rubbed against her bare legs. I wondered why humans didn't realise that they should change things if they were unhappy. She should have kicked Joe out, as he clearly didn't make her full of joy. As she bent down to fuss me, I licked her nose affectionately. She giggled, which was a welcome sound in what had been a laugh-free house, lately.

Claire was in a bad way. She looked like the Claire who had moved in here; thin and pale, with dark-ringed eyes and a taut mouth.

'Breakfast ready?' Joe asked, appearing at the kitchen door in a pair of jogging trousers and a scruffy T-shirt.

'Nearly, sit down and I'll bring it in.' She dished up one plate of food and took it into the living room, where she put it on the small dining table. He sat down and started eating without a word of thanks.

'You not having any?' he asked, finally noticing she was still standing there. She sat down with her mug.

'No, just coffee. I'm not hungry.'

'Good girl, don't want you getting fat, do we?' he said with a sneer, and he turned back to his food. I was constantly surprised by the way this awful man seemed to become more and more terrible every day, especially when my Claire was so lovely. His plate was piled high, and he had no manners. As egg yolk dripped down his chin, he wiped it away with his hand. Looking at Claire, I could see that she clearly couldn't cope with his behaviour. My heart was breaking again, but I still didn't know what to do.

A few hours later, when Claire had cleaned all the dishes, given me some fried egg (which I really liked), and tidied the house, Joe appeared from upstairs, dressed in jeans and a shirt.

He looked smarter; normal almost. But of course I'd seen the real him.

'Are you going out?' Claire asked, her voice barely a whisper.

'I told you, it's Garry's birthday and we're going bowling and then out.'

'Oh, sorry, I'd forgotten.'

'Yeah, well don't wait up.'

'Have fun.' Claire smiled at him but he didn't smile back.

'Sure. Oh, by the way, you couldn't lend me £30? Just for a few days? Work still haven't paid what they owe me, but they said they would definitely put it in this week.' I knew this was a lie. Joe had been taking money from Claire for ages and not giving her anything back. I wanted to scratch and bite him but I knew that would only make things worse.

Claire went to get her purse and came back with three notes. She handed them over and Joe took them, without a glance. He pocketed them without thanks and he didn't even kiss her goodbye as he left the house. Claire watched him go as if she didn't understand what was happening to her, and I really don't think she did. I was pretty sure she didn't know how this man, who had been so charming to her at first, was now living with her, eating her food, taking her money, and not even being nice to her. Her eyes were questioning how she had got herself into this situation; but she also looked as if she had no idea what to do.

I was despairing, as Claire went upstairs, took a shower and got dressed. I followed her to offer her my support; it wasn't much, but it was all I had. She looked a little better when she was clean and dressed but she started cleaning rigorously and I could see her sadness.

I was so relieved when the doorbell rang and she opened the door to find Tasha on the other side. I rushed to Tasha and almost leapt into her arms, I was so pleased to see her. She'd hardly been round at all since Joe had moved in, and it made me very sad. I missed her terribly and I hoped she would know what to do about Claire.

'I didn't know you were coming,' Claire said, eyeing her suspiciously.

'Sorry, I was just passing. Can I come in?' she asked. Claire nodded and stood aside. Something wasn't right here. They didn't greet each other warmly like they had done previously. 'Is Joe here?'

'No, he's gone out. Coffee?' Claire asked.

'Yes please.' They walked through to the kitchen, where Claire busied herself with the kettle and the cups. 'Claire, are you OK?' Tasha asked.

'I'm fine, I'm great,' she replied, defensively.

'I haven't seen you outside work in over a month, Claire. I thought we were friends.' I saw Claire's shoulders hunch.

'We are friends, Tash, but things have been really hectic with Joe. But as I said, I'm fine.'

'You look as if you really need to eat,' Tasha said.

'I'm watching my weight, that's all.'

'There's nothing of you.'

'I like being thin.' There was a sharp edge to her voice.

'Claire, you were like this when I first met you. Your ex-husband did that to you and then you started to get over him. Do you remember how much we laughed? And you loved work and the book group and everything.'

'Look Tasha, I told you the other day, I'm fine. I'm trying to be happy. The only thing that's wrong is that Joe is having this awful time with work and I need to be supportive. He needs me.' She looked determined when she mentioned Joe.

'But you don't talk to me any more; you never come to the book group and refuse every invitation to come out. Then, when you come to work, you put your head down and avoid me. I have no idea why you're shutting me out!' Tasha seemed genuinely upset and worried. I decided to make a grand gesture; I went to her and jumped up into her arms. I wanted to convey to her that she was right and she needed to do something. I wasn't sure if she understood, but she held me as if she did.

'I'm not avoiding you, Tasha, you're just being paranoid. How many times can I say that everything is fine?' I looked at the two women; they both looked as if they were going to refuse to budge. As she gently put me back down on the floor, I crossed my paws that Tasha would make Claire see sense.

'It's not that we've even been allowed to meet Joe properly. Whenever I ask you both out, you make excuses. Is that you or him?'

'It's both of us. Joe isn't in a great place because of work, I thought you understood that I needed to support him.'

'OK, I'm going to risk you killing me, but I'm going to say it. You hardly knew Joe before he moved himself in, what was it, a month ago? He treats you like a doormat; we've all seen it. He might say that the work thing isn't his fault but do you really believe him? People don't get fired for no reason these days. If he's as innocent as he says, then he would be taking them to a tribunal.'

'He's talking to HR and lawyers at the moment, you know how long these things take,' Claire replied, although she didn't sound convinced. 'And he hasn't moved in. He's staying here because he needs my support.'

'Are you sure? From what I can gather, you're rushing home from work every day to see him.'

'Actually Tasha, I am sure. He still has his flat, and anyway, I like having him here.' She didn't sound very convincing to me. Or to Tasha either.

'Do you? Because you seem miserable to me. And to everyone at work. We're worried about you. You don't come for drinks. You never answer my texts. You look pretty bad, to be frank. So if this is your idea of happy, then God help you.' Tasha's voice was raised and her face was red. I wanted to shout in agreement but I just stood there, watching. Claire was lying, to Tasha and maybe to herself. There hadn't been a conversation as far as I knew, but it was clear that Joe had, in effect, moved in.

'Tasha, I appreciate your concern. But this is my life. After my horrible marriage I didn't think anyone would want me. But Joe does. And not only that, he needs me. This is a tough time for him, and he needs my support. I love Joe and we're happy. I don't need you or anyone else coming round and interfering.'

'I'm only doing it because I care about you. You do know that, don't you? I'm worried.' Tasha looked very sad and defeated all of a sudden.

'Please don't worry.' Claire's voice was colder than I'd ever heard her. 'I've got a lot to do today, so I'd be grateful if you left.' Claire turned away from Tasha, who slowly backed out of the kitchen. I saw Claire pour the untouched coffee down the sink before I followed Tasha outside. She leant against the front gate and I stood next to her.

'Oh Alfie, why can't she see what a user he is?' I tilted my head. She crouched down as if to have a face-to-face conversation with me. 'He's bad, you know that, I can tell, but what can we do? She just won't listen. If only you could somehow get him to show his true colours.' I tilted my head the other way, questioningly. 'You know, I've seen this before with other people. Women who change like this with men are usually being abused in some way. You must have seen more than me, Alfie, living with them. I wish you could tell me. Oh God, I'm talking to a cat.' She laughed, bitterly. 'No offence, Alfie, but I don't think you or I can solve this one.'

I hated that humans underestimated me but at the moment she was right; I could think of no way to fix this. However, since I was feeling quite confident having sorted the situation with Philippa, which I felt I could take some credit for, perhaps something would come to me. I kept playing Tasha's words in my head, 'getting him to show his true colours', and I prayed for some inspiration.

I returned through the cat flap to find Claire. She was sitting at the table in the living room and she looked very sad. I jumped up onto the table and gave her a quick cat kiss, licking her nose gently. She smiled sadly, and didn't even try to get me off her table. Things must have been bad.

'Sometimes it feels like you are the only one who doesn't judge me,' she said. I purred. I did actually judge her, but she needed my support. 'Alfie, I love you but I need to go to the supermarket. Don't worry, I'll get you a treat for supper.' She pulled herself up, and leaving me sitting on the table, she got ready to leave.

I saw Jonathan arrive back from the gym, so I went to check on him. I was hoping for some time at the number 22 flats later but I didn't want to be too far from Claire; I was so worried about her. Jonathan was on the phone and when he hung up, he smiled at me.

'I'm going out with some friends from work to celebrate my newfound freedom,' he joked. 'I'll give you some salmon before I go, but I suggest you don't wait up.' He laughed and I miaowed along with him. He then picked me up and spun me round.

'You know, Alfie, us humans are a funny bunch. I thought I wanted a relationship so much I was willing to put up with being bossed around by Philippa. But actually I'm happier without her. I can see that now!' He laughed again. If only Claire could see this. He was right, he was nicer now, so much nicer than ever before, and maybe it had taken a relationship with a rotter like Philippa for him to see the special bond I knew we shared.

I remember Margaret talking about how people grow. Sometimes they grow straight, and sometimes they take wrong turns, but humans evolve and change often. She also said that sometimes it took very bad things to make people blossom, which made little sense to me until I had my own bad things to deal with. I had been a very young cat but I'd had to grow up fast and learn hard lessons, which I hadn't always welcomed, but which would stand me in good stead for the future. Jonathan had grown too, but my poor Claire; she was wilting. I hoped it was one of the wrong turnings that Margaret had spoken about and that she would start growing straight again.

I had to make sure that my families were all right; but it was a big responsibility for a little cat.

# Chapter Twenty-Nine

Joe had returned home late that night, waking both Claire and me. He was being nice to Claire in a very horrible way, pawing at her and kissing her and I left the room before they kicked me out.

I headed back to Jonathan's for the night. I was greeted by an empty house, and, once again, Jonathan didn't come home at all. What a bunch of humans I had chosen!

I felt like a ping pong ball as I padded back over to Claire's for breakfast. Surprisingly, she and Joe were all smiles as they had breakfast together. Claire even ate a little bit, although it was only a very small amount. I saw Claire chewing her lip nervously.

'Joe, can I ask you something?' she said, sounding timid. He nodded. 'It's just that you've been here over a month now and, well, you seem to have moved in, but we haven't talked about it.' I saw his eyes darken.

'Are you saying you don't want me here?' he asked.

'No, of course not. But, well, we don't talk about your job or your flat or what's happened. Are you living with me properly?' She looked unsure and scared.

'Claire, I wanted to ask, but I was too worried you would say no. I was so ashamed, but I lost my flat. Work have messed me around with money and the lawyer who is helping me demanded payment up front. I couldn't afford the rent.' He put his head in his hands. 'I was just too afraid to tell you.' Claire looked as if she didn't understand and I could see she had no grip on this situation at all.

'If you need somewhere to live, you can move in. You only had to say. Joe, I would never judge you, I love you.'

'Oh Claire, I would love to move in here properly. I'll go and get the rest of my stuff this week!' He looked like the cat that got the cream. 'It's going to be great, and as soon as I sort work and everything out, we'll put it on a more official footing. You know, with bills and stuff.' I narrowed my eyes in confusion. How on earth had he managed to do this? I knew he was lying. He had given his flat up a couple of weeks ago and asked a friend to keep his stuff for now – I had heard the phone calls. I hoped Claire would tell him to sling his hook, like Jonathan had to Philippa. But although she looked a bit unsure, she smiled.

'Of course I want you to move in. I just wasn't sure if you already had.'

'Oh no, I'd never do that without asking you. Right, today, let's celebrate by doing something amazing.'

'There's an exhibition at The National Gallery I'm dying to see,' Claire said, tentatively.

'Then we shall go. Today is all about you, my love, so whatever you want to do, I want to do.' Joe leant over and kissed her. I hadn't seen him being like this for ages and I wondered what had brought it on. I wondered if he had noticed how bad she looked, or felt, or if he actually did care after all, although I was still highly suspicious.

'You don't know how happy that makes me,' she giggled, looking pleased.

'That's all that matters,' he replied, tightly, and I knew, deep down, that he wasn't genuine.

I took a leisurely stroll over to the number 22 flats. The sun was back again, it was a lovely day, and I felt a little bit of a spring in my step, despite the drama. When I got to the flats, both families were congregated out the front, with lots of bags. Both Franceska and Polly were in summer dresses; the men and boys wore shorts and T-shirts, and they all looked animated and happy.

'Alfie,' Aleksy shouted, coming over to me. 'We have picnics.'

'Hi Alfie,' Thomasz the man said, coming over to stroke me.

'Alfie can come too?' Aleksy asked, hopefully.

'No, we go on train, cats no go on train.'

'We go to sea,' Aleksy explained, but he looked sad that I couldn't come.

I felt disappointed too. I could have done with a change of scene. As they chatted excitedly, and organised their many bags, I smelt something very exciting. It was tuna. I loved tuna! I followed my nose and found that the biggest bag contained a blanket and some wrapped packages, which I was pretty sure contained tuna of some sort. I put my head in for a closer look and, before I knew it, I had climbed right into the bag. It was comfortable and soft and smelt so good. I breathed in the heady scent of fish, but before I had a chance to climb out again, I saw a hand – Thomasz's – pick the bag up, and put it in the car. I didn't know what to do as I felt the car start moving, so I did nothing. My first instinct was to panic, and so I nearly called out, but then I remembered I was with my families. It seemed I could go to the seaside after all.

I knew I had to keep quiet, but in the end I fell asleep anyway when we got on the train. As they put me on the floor, I curled up and the motion rocked me off to dreamland. I was vaguely aware of the train stopping, then being picked up again. There was a lot of noise as I was put down on the ground. I tentatively poked my head out but all I could see was a lot of legs. I spotted a dog sniffing around so I hid again.

After being carried, and driven, and carried again, we finally stopped. I could feel warmth overhead, and hear seagulls squawking hungrily and lots of human chatter. I heard the men talk about arranging deck chairs and Franceska said she would lay out the picnic. She opened the bag and I jumped out. I would have shouted 'surprise' if I could have. Everyone went quiet for a minute, but then Aleksy shrieked with laughter, little Thomasz joined in and even Henry giggled as I went to say 'hello' to him in his pushchair. Franceska picked me up.

'Our little stowaway.' Everyone laughed and I suddenly felt a joy that had been absent from so many of our lives lately. Yet again, I felt as if I had done the right thing for my families.

'Don't wander off, Alfie,' Matt said, quite sternly, when the laughter died down. 'We're a long way from home, so stay with us.' I looked at him indignantly. What kind of cat did he think I was?

The picnic was such fun. I sat on the edge of the blanket, blinking at the bright sun, being fed bits of food, and watching. Other people seemed to point at me a lot. Perhaps cats didn't really go to the seaside after all. I certainly didn't want to go to the water with some of the others as they went to paddle in the sea. Still remembering my pond experience, I decided to stay well away from the sea. I sat with Polly as the others went, even Henry.

Although she had seemed happy, the sadness returned to Polly's eyes when she was alone. She let me sit next to her and stroked me absently, but I wondered where she was; she wasn't sitting on the beach with me. I wondered what I could do to help her. Until I knew, I curled up into her side and tried to convey my love.

We stayed like that for a while until the others returned, dripping wet.

'Alfie!' Aleksy shook himself near me. I yelped and jumped out of the way.

'Cat's don't like water,' Matt explained, and he winked at me.

'Sorry,' Aleksy said, and I purred in forgiveness.

We passed a wonderful afternoon. Both families were happier than I had seen them. There was so much laughter and joy that my heart swelled. I could hear the birds squawking overhead. The sun was quite hot but I managed to find some shade near Henry's pushchair when it got too fierce. Aleksy and Thomasz collected stones, there was a beachful to choose from. At one point, the men went to get ice cream, and they even got one for me!

Oh, it was heavenly, as I licked my first ice cream ever. I balked at bit at how cold it was at first, wrinkling my nose and shivering, which made everyone laugh, but then I tried again and it was delicious. Really creamy! Suddenly a big seagull swooped down in front of us and looked menacingly at me. Thomasz, the little one, screamed in fright, but I stood myself up on all fours as big as I could be (although he was still bigger than me) and hissed at him fiercely. He gave me a look as if he was weighing up an attack, but I hissed again and spat and he flew off.

'Alfie very brave,' Aleksy said, and he petted me as I returned to my ice cream. I might have seemed brave to him, but I was shaking inside. I wasn't sure that I would have survived if it had descended into a fight!

'It's OK, Alfie, we would have saved you,' Thomasz the man said, although I wasn't sure if even he would have been a match for an angry, hungry seagull; they had a reputation for ruthlessness among our community.

When the sun started to sink, Franceska said it was time to go home, so the children changed into clean clothes, the rubbish was collected and the bags packed. I was told this time to travel in a bag that sat underneath Henry's pushchair. It was actually quite a comfortable way to be transported home, so I didn't mind at all. I slept most of the way dreaming of ice cream.

Bags were unloaded at the number 22 flats. I bid everyone goodbye and wearily made my way down the street back to Claire's.

'I wonder where he goes to when he leaves us? Where does he really live?' Matt said, and they all looked at me as if I should provide the answer.

# Chapter
# Thirty

The following morning, after my usual rounds, I made my way to number 22 to go and play. I really wanted to relive the pleasure of being at the seaside with them; making the boys laugh, as I had yesterday. It made my heart swell that I could bring happiness into their lives.

I was about to try to get Franceska or Aleksy's attention but I was stopped short by a noise. It was a strange noise I hadn't heard before. A bit like the sound of a cat being strangled, but it was coming from Polly's flat. Then I heard Henry screaming and more of the other noise. I was pretty sure the sound had to be coming from Polly.

I instinctively knew what I had to do. I scratched frantically and miaowed as loudly as I could before Franceska appeared at the front door.

'Oh, Alfie, come in,' she said, stepping aside, but I stood firm. She looked at me strangely. 'What do you want?' I walked next door and stood outside Polly's, miaowing. Franceska tentatively moved towards me when suddenly the loud noise was emitted again – and this time, she heard it.

'What is it?' she asked, eyes wide in horror. 'Oh God, it sounds like someone hurt.' She put her door on the latch, shouted up to Aleksy that she would only be a minute, and then we both stood outside Polly's door.

She rang the bell and hammered on the door. After what felt like ages, Polly opened it and handed Henry to Franceska.

'Take him, please take him. I can't bear it any more.' Her beautiful porcelain skin was tear-stained, her hair wild, and she looked dreadful.

'Polly,' Franceska said, gently, as she took Henry into her arms. He immediately stopped crying.

'No, take him. I can't bear it any more. I can't do it. I'm a terrible mum and I can't even love my own baby.' She collapsed onto the floor, put her head in her hands, and sobbed.

'Polly,' her voice was soft. 'I have to go and feed Henry. He is hungry.' She spoke slowly, the way people speak to animals and small children. Polly didn't reply. 'Here, I put your door on the latch, and I call Matt? You give me his number.'

'No, you can't. I can't bear it. If Matt sees me like this, he'll never forgive me. I won't give you his number.' She started wailing again. Franceska nipped into Polly's flat and came back with Henry's milk and some bottles. She picked up the bag that Polly always kept by the front door and took Henry back to her flat. But she looked terrified, as if she didn't know what to do.

She phoned Thomasz while preparing Henry's milk, but they spoke in Polish so I didn't know what they were saying. Franceska sounded a little bit hysterical and I had never seen her look so anxious as she fed Henry, and tried to settle her two boys, who seemed to sense that something was wrong. I tried to play with Aleksy to distract him, but it was as if he was too worried to have fun.

A little while later, Thomasz arrived.

'You must take her to doctor,' he instructed, after she told him a bit more about Polly. 'Now, it is emergency. I can stay here with boys. Is OK.' He put his arms around her and gave her a reassuring hug.

'What about work?'

'We were quiet today, so it's fine.'

'I am glad your boss is also friend.'

'He is fine. He understand that I work hard and that I wouldn't leave if I didn't have to.'

'I hope so.' Franceska issued instructions on what to do with the boys and Henry, who had fallen asleep and was cushioned on the sofa.

'After the doctor, we call Matt.'

'She begged me not to.'

'But she needs him, she just isn't right with her head. I think when we call him she will be pleased eventually.'

'You have his number?'

'Yes. Take her to doctor, and then when you come back we call him.'

I went with Franceska to Polly's flat, where she opened the door. Polly hadn't moved from the spot on the floor where she had collapsed earlier.

'Polly?' Franceska said softly.

'Is Henry all right?' she asked, without looking up.

'He is very good. He is fed and sleeping. You, I take you to the doctor.'

'I can't go anywhere.'

'We have to. You have baby who needs you but you are sick, and until we go to doctor then you won't be fixed.' Franceska sat down on the floor next to Polly and I sat next to her.

'You think I'm ill?' She looked at Franceska with her sad, beautiful eyes.

'I think you have baby sadness. It is very common and I think that you have it.' Polly looked up then at Franceska.

'I can get help?'

'Yes, you see doctor. He help you and then you get better and you enjoy your baby.'

'Have you had this?'

'For a while, with Aleksy. He was younger than Henry and I thought I didn't love him but it was just the depression. I took the pills and I love him more than I ever thought I could.'

'But Henry cries all the time. Sometimes I think the sound of him crying is going to make my brain bleed. And then I think I might die and sometimes, I even think that is a good thing.'

'OK, but Henry cry, babies cry. If you are happier then he will be happier.'

'I think he'd be better off with a mummy who deserves him.' More tears sprang forth.

'Polly, you are his mummy and you love him. You might not feel it now, but you do, and he loves you. With me I am the same. My mamma, she see something in me and she make me go to doctor like I am with you.'

'My mum said something at the weekend. She said I wasn't myself and she was worried. She thought that it was the move and Matt's new job that had taken its toll on me. But I couldn't tell her, I couldn't say that I didn't love my baby. What kind of monster does that make me?'

'An ill person, not a monster. I know you love him, you do, you just can't feel it because of the depression. Honestly, I understand. I felt similar when I got help. Lots of women do.' Franceska put her arm around Polly, who sank into her.

'Thank you so much. Do you know how much better that makes me feel, knowing I am not alone? But Matt—'

'He will understand. He good man. But first we go to the doctor and we get you some help.'

I watched as Franceska got Polly to her feet and then directed her to get her shoes and bag, and they left. She spoke to Polly as if she was a child and her voice was soothing. I felt better as I followed them out. Franceska locked Polly's front door behind us but hers was still on the latch, so I could freely go back to her flat.

I played with Aleksy, who seemed a bit happier, as he got toys out for us.

'Mamma,' Thomasz the little boy kept saying, and his father would give him a hug and biscuits. He, like Franceska, was quite calm and relaxed. He kept an eye on Henry, he tried to read stories to Thomasz, who was more interested in the television. At one point he fed the boys and he also gave me some fish. I wanted to stay with them and wait to see if Polly was going to be all right.

We seemed to be waiting a very long time. Even Thomasz became agitated. Henry woke up and Thomasz had to change his nappy. Then little Thomasz went into his cot for a sleep. Aleksy asked his dad many questions, but in Polish, so I couldn't really understand what was being said.

More time passed. Thomasz looked worried, but he went to prepare the special milk for Henry. He was coping with the three boys as if he'd always had them. He was largely calm, unruffled and very efficient. I hadn't really seen fathers look-ing after their children in this way before; in the cat world we don't really do 'hands on fathering'. But Thomasz was even calmer than Franceska, if that was possible. However, I could see that underneath it all he was worried. We all were. I rubbed myself against his leg for reassurance, which I felt he needed as much as the others.

It occurred to me that I had seen them all in bad places; some worse than others. Franceska's homesickness, Claire's heartbreak, Jonathan's loneliness and Polly's struggles with

Henry and her new home. The phone rang, interrupting my thoughts, and Thomasz snatched it up. He spoke for a few moments in Polish. When he hung up, he looked serious, as he dialled another number.

'Matt, it's Thomasz from next door.' There was a pause. 'Henry is fine, he is with me, but Polly is not good. Franceska took her to the doctor.' Another pause. 'No, she come home now but she needs rest and someone needs to help with Henry.' He looked agitated as Matt was clearly speaking. 'Can you come now? I will explain but it is hard. But all will be OK.'

Matt arrived fairly quickly. He immediately picked up Henry, but he looked terrible; worried and pale.

'I don't know how to thank you,' he said, as Thomasz went to make them tea.

'Is nothing. Is what friends do. But Matt, is serious with Polly. My wife found her today, well, no, Alfie found her, and she was having some breakdown, Franceska said. So we look after Henry and they go to see the doctor. It has been a long time but they come back now.'

'I'm so ashamed, I did this to her. Making her move when Henry was so young. I thought I was doing the right thing.' He had tears in his eyes.

'I know, because we did it too. My boys are a bit older but then the upheaval for them too is big. Matt, this isn't a fault. It is an illness and it happens. Franceska had something similar after Aleksy was born and it was very worrying. But she got some help and now she loves being their mamma and is happy.'

Matt had his head in his hands.

'I should have seen it coming. After that week at home she seemed so much better, and since she met Franceska she's been happier, so I just put it down to the move. And yesterday

... we all had such fun, so how could I miss it? What do I do? My job is crazy and we need it, we need the money.' He looked as if he was going to cry.

'Matt, Polly has mum who is good, yes?'

'Yes, she's great.'

'She come stay here for a few days, just to help out while Polly starts to get better.'

'That's a good idea. I'll call her now.' He looked a bit happier at the thought. 'We have a camp bed, a nice one, which we can put in Henry's room. The flat is a bit small to have someone else in, though.' He looked concerned.

'It does not matter. At least Polly have someone to take care of her.' Matt looked at Thomasz as if he had solved the problem. 'It might take time. She has pills but they have to find time to work,' Thomasz said cautiously.

'Yes, but at least she's got help. Oh thank you so much, and most of all, thank you, Alfie, I think you may have saved us.' As Matt made a huge fuss of me, I preened myself; I was proud and happy. I was doing good wherever I went, it seemed, and this may have been my most important act yet. I didn't dwell on the element of luck that had taken me to Polly's place at the right time, not when I had so much praise being heaped on me.

I had learnt from my time on Edgar Road that things weren't always simple. At first I had seemed to help Jonathan and Claire. But then, look at Claire now. I hadn't made her better. I still needed to help her; she desperately needed it. But until I figured out how on earth I would do that, I had to stay close to Polly and the family. Aleksy was very clingy with me and I knew that although he probably didn't understand fully what was going on, he could sense that something wasn't right. So I let him cling to me a little too tightly.

'You're my best friend, Alfie,' he said to me and I wanted to cry, the way humans did when they had their hearts touched. If what the men were saying was true, Polly still had a long way to go.

Franceska eventually arrived home, on her own.

'Polly is sleeping. She has pills to sleep and the doctor told her to take it now, she needs a lot of rest after … '

'After what?' Matt asked, looking concerned.

'Today she has a breakdown of sorts. She loves you and Henry but her head isn't feeling good. The doctor has given her pills to help in the short term but she must go and see someone. Counsellor. And she needs to rest and not be alone with Henry. The pressure is too much.'

'I've phoned her mum and she's coming down tomorrow,' Matt said. 'And I've taken a couple of days off work. They know that Polly is ill and we don't have family here.'

'You have us,' Franceska stated, simply.

'Yes, and I don't know what we would have done without you, thank you so much.'

'No thanks needed. You must go and take care of your wife and son, but we are here if you need anything.'

'I left so much to Polly, the least I can do now is to look after my son. Am I the worst father and husband ever?'

'No, Matt, you are working hard, it isn't easy to see. And Polly, she not want you to see her struggle, or have you worry, so it's a bad circle.'

'A vicious circle,' Matt said.

'Sorry?'

'That's how we say it, a vicious circle. Sorry, I didn't mean to correct your English.'

'No, is good. We need to learn. Look, I come with you and show you to feed Henry so he is OK. I feel I should tell you that the doctor give Polly something to stop her milk. She says the breastfeeding is making her worse. Henry is fine and he is eating food now so formula will be OK and it mean you can feed him too, and her mother. Polly needs rest a lot right now.'

'I'll see that she gets it. I still feel bad, like I buried my head in the sand and kept telling myself that it wasn't that bad, that she would snap out of it.'

'It's hard, postnatal depression is real illness, but she will get better. Now she can start. You are a good man, Matt, and she love you very much.'

I felt a little uncertain as I left the flat with Franceska, Henry and Matt. But I wanted to be there for Matt. Even if he didn't know it, it made me feel better to be by his side. So I stayed in the living room, quietly, as he fed Henry as per Franceska's instructions, and then bathed him and eventually put him down to sleep. I sat with Matt on the sofa as he came into the living room and wept like a baby. After a while, he sat up straighter.

'My falling apart won't help anyone. Come on, Alfie, I'll make us some dinner. I'm sure we have a can of tuna in the cupboard.' It was the first time I had ever dined with them but I didn't care about the food, I was just unsure that they should be left alone. I knew I couldn't really do anything, but I also thought my presence might be a comfort.

A bit later, Matt went to check on Polly; I went with him. She opened her beautiful eyes and looked at him.

'What time is it?' she asked, sleepily.

'It doesn't matter. Henry's asleep. According to the list Franceska left me, you can take another pill. You need to sleep.' Polly tried to sit up.

'Is he all right?' she asked. Her eyes filled with tears.

'Yes, he's perfect. And I know that as soon as you start getting better, you'll think that too.'

'I feel like I've failed. I'm a terrible mum, a bad wife, and I just didn't know how to stop feeling like that.'

Matt stroked her hair, gently. 'Darling, I feel I've failed you both. I should have taken better care of you, seen that you weren't yourself. I feel terrible too.'

'There's not going to be any point in us blaming ourselves or each other is there?' she asked, her eyes widening. Matt shook his head. 'Frankie said that. She said that we would do, but it wouldn't help, so we must stop it. I'm going to try. The doctor was really lovely, it was a woman and she understood, or seemed to. I didn't want to have to take anything but I know that I need the pills. I can and will get help. I'll be fine and I'll look after my baby; our baby. All I want is to be a good mother.'

'Of course you will be, darling.' Matt had tears swimming in his eyes. 'And I'm going to be here every step of the way. I love you so much, please Pol, never forget that.'

'I did forget but only because my head was so cloudy, but I know and I love you too.' He hugged her very tightly and this was the most moving scene I had ever watched between humans.

'Oh, and your mum is coming down. I'm sorry but we need her here, as I can't take too much time off work. I wish I could.'

'No, Matt, we both agreed about coming to live here for your promotion. You don't need to feel guilty about that. And having Mum here, well, that'll be such a relief.' They sat in silence for a few minutes. I lay down on the floor, suddenly feeling fatigued by the day's events; it had been so emotional.

'It was like a big black hole inside me, that's what it felt like. I wanted to take Henry somewhere and leave him. Just run away and be back to my old self. I love him, I know I do deep down, but I can't feel it. I can't feel the joy that mums talk about. It's horrible, Matt, so horrible.' She wept and he held her.

'I can't imagine what it must feel like, but I will support you whatever happens. But you need to talk to me. No matter how bad you feel, you have to tell me about it. I'm not going to leave you; I love you and I love our family. There is nothing you can do to change that.'

'You don't know how amazing it is for me to hear that. I wish I'd been a bit more honest with you. When I felt as if I was getting ill, not long after Henry's birth, and even before we came here, I felt that I needed to hide it at all costs. But it nearly cost too much.'

'Polly, I think you're amazing and brave and I know we'll get through this. It might take time but it doesn't matter. We can do it.'

'Can we go and see him? I don't want to wake him, I just want to look at him. I need to.' She burst into fresh tears.

'Come on,' Matt said, scooping her up in his arms as if she weighed as much as Henry. I was too sleepy to follow them through to the bedroom.

'It looks as if Alfie is staying with us tonight,' Matt said, as I felt myself drifting off.

'He looks so cosy, don't disturb him,' I heard Polly say as I fell fast asleep.

# Chapter
# Thirty-One

If I thought being a doorstep cat had been hectic before, I had no idea just how exhausting things would become. I had built myself a little community and everyone around me had become important to me in their different ways. But I couldn't be in four places at once.

Back and forth I went, trying to keep my eye on everyone who needed me, and it seemed that everyone did.

It wasn't too long a walk between all my homes but I seemed to do it a lot. I was a fit cat, but at times I did find the trek a little bit tiring. When I arrived at the flats, I found Franceska and Matt outside with the boys. They were playing on the grass, just as they had done previously with Polly. As usual, Aleksy greeted me as if I was his best friend. Franceska and Matt had mugs in their hands. Henry was lying on his tummy on the blanket, and Thomasz was looking at a book. Aleksy started to tickle me and I rolled on my back for him.

'She's been asleep on and off since she came back from the doctor yesterday. I hope it's helping,' Matt was saying.

'It will help her. She is so tired that part of the depression is exhaustion. Like you say, is vicious circle.' Franceska and Matt laughed, sadly.

'I'm going to get her mum from the train station later. Having her here will make a big difference I think, but then, she can't stay with us forever.'

'Matt, she won't need to. Polly will get better, and quicker than you think.' I felt tears in my cat eyes at the thought of the beautiful fragile woman, but I hoped Franceska was right. She would get better.

Before the breakdown, I had thought she was improving. She had seemed much brighter. But then before Joe, Claire had seemed better too. I was learning that with humans, like food, you were best off taking nothing for granted.

After a bit more playing, Franceska organised lunch for the boys and Matt joined her. He said he didn't want to disturb Polly, but I could also see he was anxious and didn't seem to want to be on his own.

'You make the formula for Henry and I mash some vegetables,' Franceska said.

'Are you sure you don't mind?'

'Don't be silly. I make vegetables for my boys and then mash them for Henry. Is easy. Is easy, if we all eat together anyway. I have soup for us? Is a Polish, um, beetroot borscht?'

'I've never had it.' Matt looked a bit dubious.

'Thomasz make it at his restaurant, is very good. You try?'

'Of course, I'd love to try it.' Matt was very polite but I wasn't convinced by his tone. And when I saw the colour of this bright red stuff, I wasn't sure about it either. Luckily, Franceska had sardines for me.

After lunch, they all went out for a walk, and then Franceska took Henry, so that Matt could go and check on Polly before collecting her mother from the train station. I stayed a bit longer to play with the boys. Thomasz was getting more and more interested in me now, copying his older brother, so it was doubly exhausting. By the time I scratched at the door to be let out, I was tired from all the playing, full from my sardines. For once, the walk back to my other homes was a good thing.

I went to check on Claire first, as I was pretty sure Jonathan wasn't home from work yet. I realised, as I entered through the cat flap, that I had become scared of this house; my fur was standing on end. It wasn't a nice feeling. Claire had been my first owner and she had made me so welcome that to feel I was intruding in my own home unnerved me. Claire was in the kitchen, but she had clearly been crying as she turned to me.

'Alfie, you're here at last!' She picked me up. 'I was beginning to get worried, it's been nearly two days. Honestly Alfie, I wish I knew where you went when you're not here. Have you got a girlfriend?' Claire asked. I miaowed, guiltily. 'Let's get you some food. I know that you're a cat and you like to go out and about, but remember that I worry about you if I don't see you.' She spoke softly but I felt as if I was being told off. I miaowed, trying to tell her that if she got rid of Joe I wouldn't be so nervous about coming home, but I knew that she wouldn't understand me. I nuzzled into her neck to say sorry instead.

'What's all the racket?' Joe asked, coming into the kitchen. He was dressed as usual, in jeans and a T-shirt, but I also noticed he was getting a bit thicker around his stomach. The thinner Claire got, the fatter he got.

'Alfie's back. I'm just going to feed him,' she said putting me down and getting some cat food out of the cupboard.

'You treat that cat better than you treat me,' he said, sounding angry.

'Don't be silly,' Claire replied, laughing.

'Don't bloody laugh at me,' he shouted, suddenly. I recoiled, as did Claire.

'I'm not—' she began.

'You are. And you know what, I've had enough. You treat me like a fool. Just because I lost my job, through no fault of my own, you think you can walk all over me.' I literally curled myself into a ball near the kitchen cupboards. I was frightened but I had no idea what to do. After Joe's previous attempts to hurt me, I wasn't sure just what he was capable of. He started to loom towards us and then seemed to change his mind; he turned around and punched the wall. It was a sudden, violent move and Claire screamed. He hadn't hit her or me, but he frightened us both. There was silence for a while.

'Joe, I think you ought to leave,' Claire said, her voice quivering. I uncurled myself and almost jumped for joy. Joe's face darkened, then suddenly it seemed to change.

'I'm sorry, gosh I'm so sorry.' He rubbed his hand. 'I just lost my temper; I've never done that before.' He moved towards Claire, who shrank further back. I went to stand protectively in front of her. I wanted to tell Claire he was a liar, but I couldn't.

'Joe, you've put a great big hole in my wall, and you say you didn't mean to lose your temper?' she pointed out. She sounded scared, not angry.

'Oh God, I'm sorry. What have I done?' Then to my amazement, he started to cry.

'Joe, don't cry,' Claire said, softening.

'I'm sorry. What must you think of me? Claire, I never behave like this but I am just so upset by the whole job thing, the fact I've lost my flat and I feel like I'm totally sponging off you.'

'But I don't mind. I know it's not forever; you'll soon get another job and be back on your feet.' Her voice was no longer angry; he was so good at manipulating her. I was losing hope.

'I wish. There's a recession. No one is hiring at the moment. I might get some freelance work but I feel like a complete loser. I had a good job, and now look at me.'

'Joe,' Claire said, and went over to him. She put her arms around him, to my despair and disgust. 'I love you, and I'm here to support you in whatever way you need. Now stop being silly and never lose your temper like that again.' It was funny to hear Claire sounding as if she was a bit more in control, but I was furious that she had forgiven him so easily. He was clearly going to lose his temper again; men like him always did. And he didn't make her happy. She must be mad if she thought he did.

'I promise, Claire, I love you so much, I'll make it up to you, I promise.'

'You can start by fixing the wall.' She laughed, weakly.

I stalked out in an unnoticed protest, and went to Jonathan's. He had obviously been home from work for a while, as he already had his gym clothes on.

'Oh, there you are, I wondered where you'd got to. I guess you've been flirting with female cats.' I miaowed but wanted to say, 'Actually, no. I've been in the presence of a madman who frightened me and I would very much like you to go and sort him out.'

'Anyway, have some dinner and then you can have a rest. Flirting is hard work.' I purred. 'High five,' Jonathan said, and I looked at him blankly. 'You know, you put your hand, or paw, up and I'll do the same.' I raised my paw and he tapped it with his hand. 'You clever cat, you learnt to do your first trick. I knew I was right to get rid of Philippa rather than you,' he laughed. I looked at him in surprise. Raising my paw got such a response? It wasn't as if I'd actually spoken or even danced. Honestly, humans could be so happy with so little.

Jonathan and I dined together before he left. I didn't feel like going out again. I was incredibly tired from my day, both physically and emotionally, so I sought out my cashmere blanket and lay down to rest. I played the events over in my mind, and I felt that I was getting there. Franceska and her family were all right and in comparison to the others they were not going to face anything too major. That was my take on it anyway. Polly, although still ill, was going to get better. I was pretty sure of that. And Jonathan, well, he was still alone in the big house, apart from yours truly, but he seemed upbeat. I really liked him now. So that left me with Claire.

I had seen how frightening Joe could be first hand today. And I knew that it wasn't going to be an isolated incident. I thought he would definitely lash out again. And next time, it would be Claire he hurt. I was sure of it.

The idea of that brute hurting my Claire upset me so much. He obviously had some kind of hold over her and I didn't know where it would lead but instinctively I knew it wouldn't be good. When would it end? I had no idea, but it had to. I felt instinctively that there must be something I could do to make it stop; I just wasn't yet sure what. As I drifted off to sleep on my soft, lovely blanket I said a cat prayer that an answer would come to me, and soon, before it was too late.

# Chapter
# Thirty-Two

I awoke knowing the answer. It was still dark outside but the dawn chorus was about to start. No wonder cats chased and killed birds, the racket they made first thing in the morning really was unnecessary. I looked over at a sleeping Jonathan. He looked so peaceful, so content. Although inside I felt terror at what was to come, I tried to be comforted by his presence.

It was going to be a risk, I knew that. My plan, which had somehow formulated in my sleep, was foolhardy to say the least. But I also knew that it was what I had to do, which meant taking the chance and hoping with every ounce of my cat being that this plan worked out.

I nestled into Jonathan. One thing I knew was that today everything would change and I wanted him to know that I loved him no matter what. He slept soundly with me by his side for a while before his clock started beeping and he sat up. I jumped up onto his chest and smiled at him again.

'Alfie, what are you doing in my bed?' he asked, but not unkindly. I miaowed. He laughed, patted me affectionately and then got out of bed.

I managed to get downstairs but my legs were feeling a little bit weak. I had never thought of myself as a brave cat. Let's face it, when I first lived with Margaret and Agnes I was anything but brave, and then when Agnes decided to like me I had no need to be brave. But when I lost them both, there was a courage that reared up in me; one I had no idea I possessed, and that's how I survived. So my legs might not feel brave, but my resolve didn't waver.

I waited in the kitchen for Jonathan to come downstairs, and when he did, he made coffee, poured me some milk, put some toast on and gave me some cold salmon that he'd cooked. I savoured the breakfast, as I realised it might be my last for a while.

'Right, Alfie, I'm off, but I'll see you after work,' Jonathan said, standing up. I crossed my paws that he would.

I set off to see Claire. When I arrived, she looked as if she hadn't slept. She was distracted as she patted me and I could see in her eyes that she was scared too. She wasn't happy with Joe, anyone could see that, but she also seemed to think that being alone was a bad thing. I had heard about this with humans, that some people would rather be with someone, even if they weren't happy, than on their own. Claire was one of those people, I'd decided. But seeing her, the state she was in, and then looking at the hole still glaring out from the wall, made me even more determined to see my plan through.

I left the house with Claire, who was going to work. I walked a little way down the street with her until she had to turn off.

'You take care, Alfie, and I'll see you tonight.' I rubbed against her leg and knew she definitely would.

It was time to take my shaky legs to the flats at number 22, where I scratched at the door before Franceska let me in.

'Alfie,' Aleksy and Thomasz said in unison and they proceeded to make a big fuss of me. I was affectionate with both boys and they rewarded me by tickling my tummy as I lay on my back. They didn't seem to mind doing this for ages and I lapped up all the wonderful sensations while I could. I played with them until Franceska said it was time to go and see Polly. I hadn't seen Polly since that day with the doctor so I was pleased to go too.

The lady that answered the door wasn't Polly but an older lady, quite elegant and not as old as Margaret.

'Franceska, how nice to see you,' she said, smiling.

'Hi, Val. We just want to see how is Polly. If there is anything we can do?'

'Yes, you can come in, she would love to see you, and the boys can entertain Henry.' She stepped aside and I followed them into the flat. 'Oh hello, you must be Alfie, the hero cat.' I purred. I decided I liked this woman.

Polly was wearing her pyjamas but she looked beautiful and a little better. Franceska gave her a big hug as the boys went straight to where Henry was sitting on his play mat, surrounded by cushions.

'Frankie, it's so nice to see you,' Polly said. 'Now I've slept for so long, I'm feeling a bit better.'

'Good, but you take time.'

'I'll pop the kettle on, shall I?' Polly's mum asked.

'Thank you, Mum.'

'I can help?' Franceska asked.

'No, love, you sit and keep my daughter company.' She left the room.

'So, are you OK, Frankie?'

'We very good. Aleksy start his school next week and I find nursery for Thomasz. Is good for him to meet children and also I get a part-time job. Just a shop or something but good for me.'

'Actually that sounds great. Improve your English, meet people. I never asked what you did in Poland, for work?'

'My family had a grocery shop, so I worked there. Not so exciting but I like. I like serving people and having chats.'

'Aleksy?' Polly said. He turned round. I was surprised; it

was the first time I had heard Polly talk directly to him, but I guess she didn't know that.

'Yes?' he said.

'Yes, Polly,' his mum corrected.

'Sorry. Yes, Polly.' Polly laughed.

'Are you excited about your new school?'

'I am yes, so, but I am also a bit scared.'

'Right, well, I think that we should go to the shops and you can choose a cool school bag and pencil case; it'll be a starting school present from Matt and me.'

'Wow, really? I can have Spiderman?'

'Whatever you want.'

'Polly,' Franceska started.

'No, please, Frankie. I can never repay what you've done and I hope you don't need me in the way I needed you, but let me treat the boys. And also, I need an outing some time soon, I can't fester in here forever. A trip to buy a Spiderman bag might do me the world of good.'

'OK, thank you.'

Val returned with the tea and they all chatted like old friends. The boys played with both Henry and me and I felt emotional as I knew what was happening next. But although I was leaving them, I knew they would be all right. They were happy, and while Polly wasn't exactly back to normal, she was at least more cheerful than she'd been. I could tell when she picked Henry up and kissed him. I had never seen her do that before. Henry barely cried the whole time I was there. It felt as if a miracle had happened in the flats at number 22.

Before lunch, they decided to take a walk to the park.

'I need some fresh air,' Polly said. 'Let me quickly throw on some clothes.' That was a curious expression, I thought, but she returned wearing jeans and a T-shirt. They started getting their shoes on. Henry was strapped into his smaller pushchair and Thomasz insisted on walking. They set off, and they turned round to me as I stood at the gate.

'Bye, Alfie,' Aleksy said.

'Bye, Alfie,' Thomasz mimicked. Both Polly and Franceska bent down to stroke me.

'If you come back at lunch time, I'll buy you some fish on our way back,' Polly said. I miaowed with joy.

'You'd swear he understood you!' Val pointed out.

'He very clever cat,' Franceska replied. 'Of course he understood.'

I rushed to see Tiger after leaving. I took the back way, which was slightly quicker; jumping fences and dodging snarling dogs. When I arrived, she was sunning herself in the back garden. I told her immediately of my plan and she looked stricken. She actually yowled at me in annoyance, but I tried to explain the thinking behind it. She called me all kinds of cat names, telling me I was an idiot. Then she cried out and said she was scared for me because we didn't know how it would turn out. She said I was a very brave, very stupid cat indeed. And I couldn't do anything but agree with her. We eventually had an affectionate goodbye and I promised that I would do whatever I could to make sure I came back to her in one piece.

I tried to forget about the visit with Tiger and what lay in store as I hastened back to number 22 for my fish.

'We go to my flat,' Franceska said, as I met her outside with the boys. 'Henry is sleeping and Val makes Polly rest too, so I have your fish.' I purred with pleasure and followed them up the stairs.

Aleksy put the television on, and Thomasz sat on the floor as close to it as he could get. Franceska, who was in the kitchen, shouted, 'Too close, Thomasz, move.' And she laughed. I wondered if she could see through walls. Cats have wonderful sight and can sense objects but even we can't do that. I followed her into the kitchen and waited for my lunch. As promised, she cooked me some fish and then served it. It was like being a human, apart from the fact that I ate from the floor. I ate quickly and then cleaned myself as she fed both the boys and herself.

After lunch she put a reluctant Thomasz down for a nap and spent time reading with Aleksy.

'Is hard to read English,' he complained.

'Yes but you are doing good. Soon you will be better than your mamma.'

'Will I like school?' he asked, looking worried.

'You will love it, just like you did in Poland.'

'But with different language.'

'Yes and the teachers say they will be very kind to you and help you, so you must not worry.' I could see that, for all her reassurances, Franceska was concerned about her boy.

'And if Polly buys me a bag, I will be very happy.' Aleksy squirmed as his mum kissed him and cuddled him.

After reading for a while, Aleksy got out his toy cars and tried to make me chase them. I did, but my stomach wasn't feeling good. My nerves were growing and although I tried to make the game fun, my heart wasn't really in it. I told myself off. If this was to be our last play for a while, or, I shuddered at the thought, even longer, then the least I could do was to have fun. So I let Aleksy push the car, which I chased and then tried to roll it back to him with my little paw. It wasn't that easy. He laughed with glee when I did this. We played for what felt like a very long time, before I had to leave. It was time for me to go and put the very scary plan into action.

As I bade everyone goodbye I memorised their faces and hoped sincerely that I would see them again soon.

# Chapter
# Thirty-
# Three

My legs were shaking as I approached Claire's house. Tiger was waiting for me outside and she gave me a quick nuzzle and wished me luck. She asked me to reconsider but I said I couldn't; something told me that this had to be done for the good of Claire, whom I loved so much. I might have been angry with her, I might have been annoyed at how weak she was, but I loved her and she needed me. I felt as if I was all she had and although that didn't feel like much, I hoped that now it would be enough for her.

I leapt with more energy than I felt through the cat flap and stood still for a moment. I could sense that Claire wasn't home yet. Joe was in the living room watching television. I took a breath and felt my fur stand on end. I remembered last feeling this level of terror when I first started being a homeless cat. My little cat heart was beating so fast that it was almost jumping out of my body.

I sat outside the living room, waiting. I wasn't sure how long I was there before I heard Claire walking down the path and I thanked God for giving us cats such excellent hearing. Timing was everything. I ran into the living room and jumped straight up onto Joe's lap. He looked surprised and then, as I had guessed he would be, angry.

'Get off me you stupid moggy,' he shouted and I hissed at him before lashing out and scratching his arm. I closed my eyes, as I had predicted what would follow.

'You stupid bloody cat, I hate you,' he said, as he threw me across the room. I curled myself into a tight ball and when I felt myself falling, I put my legs out and landed straight. Claire had entered the house, so I yowled as loudly as I could.

Joe darted across the room and began to kick me repeatedly. The pain seared through my entire body, and I could no longer even cry out.

'Oh my God, what the hell, get off him, get the hell off him, you bastard!' I heard Claire cry before everything went black.

I wasn't sure, despite watching lots of hospital dramas with Margaret, whether I was conscious, unconscious or something in between. I knew I wasn't dead because I hadn't seen Agnes or Margaret and I was pretty sure that in death I would. I was warm though, although it felt as if we were moving as the pain seared through me. I could vaguely hear voices and was reassured that one of them was Claire's.

'What have I done?' she cried. 'I let him use me and now he's gone and nearly killed Alfie. Oh God, if he dies, I'll never forgive myself.'

'Claire,' it was Tasha's voice I could now make out. 'You were vulnerable after the divorce. We thought you were better but that wasn't real, was it? You still felt worthless and I should have seen that. But Joe, well he did see it. Men like him sense these things. You can't blame yourself. Look, Alfie will be OK, we're nearly at the vet and I know he's going to make it through.' But she didn't sound sure, I could hear it in her voice. 'And he saved you.'

'You know, Alfie watched him punch a wall the other day. I bet he thought he would have done it to me next.'

'He would have done if you hadn't kicked him out.'

'I know that now. When he was kicking a poor defenceless cat I suddenly woke up and finally found the strength I never thought I had. I pulled him away, I was so angry that I shoved him and hit him myself, but then he started to do the whole "sorry" thing. Unbelievable! This time, I wouldn't have it. I told him if he didn't get out in five minutes I'd call the police.'

'What did he do?'

'He cried, just like when he punched the wall, but I stood firm. I was too scared to pick Alfie up, which is why I called you. There was blood everywhere and he wasn't moving. Joe was still standing there, not going anywhere, so I told him to get out again, and then he got nasty. So with the phone in my hand I dialled 999 and told him: one more step and I'd press the call button.'

'And that was when he finally left?'

'Yes, but not before calling me all the filthy names under the sun.'

'He was horrible.'

'But why didn't I see it?'

'I don't know, if I'm honest. I thought he controlled you. But then when you want something badly enough, you only see what you want to see. Claire, you have to learn from this; there are, unfortunately, lots of men like Joe out there.'

'I am so sorry and stupid and I'll never forgive myself if anything happens to Alfie.'

'That sort of attitude, calling yourself stupid, got you into the mess in the first place.' I could hear that Tasha was being very real with Claire, which I liked, and Claire was crying, which I didn't like, but as I drifted off back to the blackness, there was very little I could do about anything any more.

My plan had worked, I had got rid of Joe at last. I just hoped the cost wasn't too high.

# Chapter
# Thirty-Four

I don't know how many days had passed in this strange place. I was in an animal hospital, where the vet had done various things to me. He said I had to stay there, as I was barely conscious. I vaguely heard talk of an operation and I had been given injections that made the blackness come. I could hear voices, but not always make out what they were saying. I was being given pain medication that took the pain away, but left me feeling drowsy. I wasn't scared any more because I didn't have the energy for such emotions. I felt as if I was mainly sleeping. But not normal sleep, with fish-filled dreams, but sleep where nothing happened and nothing was going to happen.

One day I woke up and opened my eyes. I flicked my whiskers, which were still there. Although I couldn't quite move, I felt my brain was a bit more normal again.

'Alfie,' a woman said. I looked at her. She wore a green coat and had her hair tied back. She seemed kind, though. 'I'm Nicole, one of the nurses who have been looking after you. It's good to see your eyes finally. The vet will be along to see you in a minute.'

And then I knew I was getting better. The vet prodded and poked me and I hissed at him but he laughed at that. Nicole stroked me and then said I was well enough for Claire to come and visit me now.

I nearly cried with happiness when Claire arrived with Tasha to see me. It was a bit of a struggle to keep my eyes open but I did, just long enough to see her looking much better as she had done after her weekend away; more like her pre-Joe self.

'Oh, Alfie, they told me you're going to be all right,' she cried, tears streaming down her cheeks, but tears of happiness, I presumed.

'Thank goodness, you're looking more like your cute self again. This has been the longest week of my life,' Claire said, 'but if you carry on like you're doing, then in another week, you could be home with me again.'

'And don't worry, there is no Joe any more,' Tasha said.

'No, he's long gone and no one else will ever come between us. You saved me, Alfie, I know you did.'

'Don't you think it's weird?' Tasha said.

'What?' Claire asked.

'That it happened the way it did?'

'What do you mean?'

'Well it's almost as if he planned it. Joe punches a wall and scares you both, then a day or so later, you come in from work and find him kicking your cat.'

'Because he's a brute and I still hate to think about it,' Claire snapped.

'But no, I mean, he claimed that Alfie attacked him, right? Well what if he did? What if he provoked Joe to make sure that he would never hurt you?'

'I know Alfie's clever, but he's not that clever. Tash, are you crazy? He's a cat.'

I smiled to myself as I drifted back to sleep.

Claire visited a lot over the next few days and I regained my strength. I could stand up again, as nothing had been broken, thankfully, although I still felt pain and the vet said I might not be as agile as I once was. But I didn't care, because I could still walk, and although I had internal injuries, I had apparently been a very lucky cat. I didn't feel it at the time, or afterwards, but maybe I had been.

A few days before I was due to go home, Claire arrived again, but not with Tasha this time. I was awake but very drowsy, having just had some medication, and I couldn't easily open my eyes. But the voice I heard was unmistakable.

'Alfie!' he cried. 'God, what happened to you?' My Jonathan! I tried, but failed, to open my eyes.

'So, you're saying Alfie's your cat?' Claire sounded annoyed.

'I told you he was my cat! I've been bloody looking every-where for him.'

'I saw your posters but I didn't think it could be the same cat, because he's mine,' Claire stated.

'What, despite the posters saying that I was missing a little grey cat called Alfie?' Jonathan's voice was angry as it had been when I first met him.

'Well, yes, I can see how you might think that now.' Claire sounded slightly contrite.

'So, despite the fact that he looks exactly the same and has the same name, you still thought it was a different cat?' I was glad Jonathan clearly hadn't been changed by my absence.

'Well, I mean, he's my cat.'

'So you say, but how many cats called Alfie that look like him do you think there are in one street in London?' I could hear the impatience in his voice.

'I just didn't … I'm sorry, he must be living with both of us.'

'I guess it explains why he disappears so much.'

'I always wondered about that,' Claire said.

'I can't believe I've been putting those posters up for over a week and you didn't even think to call me.'

'I only saw it the other day, and then, as I keep saying, I

didn't think it could be the same cat. So tonight, when I actually saw you putting up more posters I finally clicked, didn't I?' Claire didn't sound as much a pushover as usual. She was standing up to Jonathan, which amused me.

'I've been worried sick.'

'Of course, I understand and I'm sorry. I mean it. But I did think he was my cat!' I tried to miaow to remind them that I was there, but no sound came out.

'And what about the kid?' My ears pricked up. Did they mean Aleksy? I was beginning to feel loved. Jonathan had missed me and had been looking for me and maybe the families at number 22 were too?

'Look, I honestly only saw your poster. I didn't see the other one, with the drawing of a cat on it, until you showed me.' Claire sounded flustered now. 'And even if I had, I'm not sure the picture of the cat looked anything like my Alfie,' she tried a weak laugh.

'The kid, or I guess it's a kid, unless it's a very incompetent adult who drew it, must be really upset.'

'I know and I feel bad but I didn't know quite what a flirt Alfie was!' She laughed. 'He must have been getting fed everywhere.'

'Yes, I'm guessing that this little monkey of a cat was pretty well fed and looked after. That's three houses that we know of. Goodness knows how many more there might be. Look, let's go see the kid when we leave here. If they're anything like me, they'll be worried sick about Alfie.'

'I really am sorry.'

'If I ever see the bastard that did this to Alfie, I'll kill him. Who could do that to a defenceless cat? What total, utter scum.' Darkness clouded Jonathan's face.

'I know and I wish I'd called the police or something. I feel so responsible and terrible for letting it happen to him.'

'I suppose it's not your fault entirely,' Jonathan said, not thawing all the way, but perhaps sounding slightly less angry.

'It is. That's the problem, it's completely my fault.'

'It can't have been easy for you, having to see him get hurt,' Jonathan conceded. Claire burst into tears. Managing to open one eye, I saw Jonathan pat her awkwardly on the shoulder and it suddenly struck me how good they looked together; albeit a bit blurry through my sleepy eyes.

'I'm sorry, Jonathan.'

'Don't be. He's going to be all right.' I saw Claire nod her head.

'Oh Alfie,' Claire said, reaching in to stroke me through the bars of my cage. 'It seems that you are one very loved cat.'

I knew then that my recovery would be swift, because I was loved and I loved each and every one of them too. And besides, I had a new, and hopefully far less dangerous, plan to occupy myself with now.

# Chapter
# Thirty-Five

Chapter
thirty-five

It was the day to go home and I was so excited. No more cage, not that it was that bad, but it was hardly The Ritz. And although they had encouraged me to exercise, I had been confined. Now I would go back to my life of wandering the length of Edgar Road, perhaps not quite jumping the fences as I used to, but having a go at the very least. I was so looking forward to seeing all my families and Tiger too, although I wasn't sure if they were cross with me now they had all discovered each other. I hoped not.

Claire came to collect me and although I wasn't happy about it, she and the vet bundled me into my cat basket. I screeched, not with pain, but because I find it very undignified being shoved into one of those.

'He really ought to be kept in one place for a while. I would recommend that he exercise, but gently. He should be able to figure it out, but I want him kept in for at least one more week and then I'd like you to bring him in for a check-up,' the vet instructed. I tried to scowl at her from the cat carrier; that didn't sound like fun and it wasn't what I had planned.

'Don't worry, I'll take good care of him.'

Jonathan stood at the desk, waiting for both Claire and me. I was delighted to see him.

'I just need to pay the bill,' Claire said, as the lady on the desk handed it to her.

'Jesus,' Jonathan said, whistling. 'Bloody expensive.'

'Well, as he's your cat too, maybe you'd like to chip in,' Claire said. Jonathan looked shocked, but then Claire laughed.

'Only joking. I have insurance.'

'You have insurance?' Jonathan asked, incredulously, as if he'd never heard of it.

'Yes, Alfie is my cat and so of course I have him insured.'

'Never occurred to me,' Jonathan said.

'Well that doesn't surprise me,' Claire retorted. 'I bet you forget to feed him if you go away as well, don't you?' Jonathan had the grace to look bashful, because he did.

'Well, with four homes, I'm sure he never goes hungry.'

'Not the point. Right, let's get going, we've got a party to go to.' I felt indignant myself then, they were having a party on my first day back?

Jonathan parked his car outside his house and he carried me in, with Claire following behind. They had bickered about me the entire journey home, until I was sure that it was only a matter of time before they realised they were meant for each other. Perhaps it wasn't immediately obvious, because they were arguing and Claire had just got out of a volatile relationship, but actually, to me, they made perfect sense. Their arguing was different; softer, and not as aggressive. Not only that, but Claire gave as good as she got. She wasn't timid around him. She was the Claire I knew she should be. Call it cat's intuition, but I just knew in my heart that these two could love each other as much as I loved them.

I was growing happier by the minute. Especially with thoughts of prawns and my cashmere blanket, of Aleksy and our ball games, of seeing how Polly was, and Henry and the two Thomaszes, and of course, not forgetting my lovely Franceska. Oh, how I had missed them, I thought, as I smiled broadly and waited to be let out of the cat carrier.

Jonathan put me down in the hallway and opened the

door. He picked me up and carried me to the kitchen. I was still upset that they were leaving me to go to a party but as the door opened, I miaowed in surprise.

'Alfie,' Aleksy shouted, and ran over. He stopped just in front of Jonathan. There was a colourful banner pinned to the wall, and around Jonathan's kitchen table were Franceska, the two Thomaszes, Matt, Polly and Henry. I couldn't believe it. These people didn't know each other and here they were, all together.

'You've been rumbled, Alfie,' Matt laughed.

'What is rumbled?' Aleksy asked.

'We found out he have four homes, well, not that he lives with us, but he visits us,' Franceska laughed.

'Yes, Alfie, we look for you and I draw picture but we no find you and we worry. But then they tell us you were hurt.' Aleksy looked tearful.

'Here, Aleksy, if you're very gentle, you can hold him.' Jonathan passed me to Aleksy who kissed me. Claire had joined us. It was so funny seeing all my families here together. I studied them while I nestled into Aleksy. Polly looked more gorgeous than ever and definitely much better as she bounced Henry on her lap. Thomasz and Matt looked the same. Franceska looked as in control as ever, and little Thomasz looked as if he had grown in my absence. But Claire looked wonderful. I had seen her at the vet's but not really taken her in. She was beginning to blossom again; she seemed to have put on a little bit of weight – I noticed these things – and her cheeks were gaining colour. She was beautiful, I thought, as was Jonathan.

Jonathan took me from Aleksy and put me in the bed that was usually at Claire's house. They put my food down next to me: salmon and prawns, the best meal ever.

They made a fuss of me and everyone gave me presents. It was like it was my birthday! Aleksy and Thomasz had drawn me pictures, which were of a cat and a car. The children had been told that I had been hit by a car whilst crossing the road, so that they weren't distressed by what had really happened. I minded slightly, I had crossed half of London dodging traffic, for goodness sake, I think I knew my Green Cross Code.

'You must be careful crossing the road,' Aleksy said to me, and Jonathan winked.

'There's one last present,' Jonathan said.

'Long overdue,' Claire added. She reached over to me and gently removed my collar. She took off the tag that tied me to Margaret. She held up a new one and everyone clapped. 'Alfie, this has your name and all of our phone numbers etched on it. All four of your families, so you'll never be lost again.'

People say cats can't cry but I promise you, I had tears swimming in my eyes.

I was exhausted, but they were being gentle and loving with me, everyone saying how much they'd missed me. My heart swelled so much I thought it would outgrow my body. Seeing all my families sitting around at Jonathan's house was the best present ever.

They talked about a rota. I was to stay at Claire's whilst I was getting better, and she had taken some time off work to nurse me. Then Jonathan said he had taken different days off to take care of me too. Apparently I needed my medicine regularly, and I needed to be quiet.

'There's a sweet cat that seems to have been looking for you too,' Claire said. 'The one who lives next door to me.' I wondered if Tiger would come and visit me as well. That would complete my friends and family.

Eventually, when Aleksy was promised he could visit me after school, and Polly said she would bring Henry round and sit with me when Claire had to go to the shops, and each and every one of them had kissed me and petted me gently, they all left.

Jonathan carried me back to Claire's house and settled me downstairs. They said I wasn't up to managing the stairs yet and I felt quite weak, so I guessed they were right.

'Will you stay for a drink?' Claire asked him, when I had curled up to rest.

'Of course. Do you fancy getting a takeaway too? I'm famished. I mean, only if you want the company,' Jonathan said, and I was pretty sure he turned a bit red as he suggested this.

'That would be great. I'm so glad he's home,' she replied, looking down at me.

'Well, one of his homes anyway,' Jonathan replied and they both laughed. My heart lifted as I heard in their voices something I often felt in mine; love. They might not know it yet but I did. I was a very clever cat.

# Epilogue

I was visiting Tiger. She was trying to exercise more with me, having acknowledged that she needed to lose some weight. She said that when I'd been away she had eaten and not moved much, pining for me, which was nice, although I think she was just being a bit lazy as she was prone to.

Many months had passed since *the incident*, such as it had now become known. I hadn't realised that although my plan was dangerous and had nearly caused my death – I wasn't quite aware of how near death I'd been – the outcome had been better than I could ever have envisaged. But, as the seasons passed, my strength had returned. It was now summer again. The sun was out, the evenings light and warm. I had survived it all; the attack by Joe, and the cold winter that followed, which made me loath to go out. I had eventually forced myself to set foot outside the front door, returning to my old life of visiting all the houses; Jonathan's, the flats at number 22, and of course, Claire's. After my recovery I had returned to being a doorstep cat but with a difference, because everything was different. And now things had changed more than ever.

Franceska and Thomasz and the boys had moved and left Edgar Road. Luckily they had only gone round the corner though, and lived in a bigger flat. I didn't visit often, as it was quite a walk, but they came to Polly and Matt's or Jonathan and Claire's all the time. It seemed that I had brought about a friendship for all of my families, which made me so happy; they liked each other, just as I had wanted.

Thomasz had a partnership in his restaurant and was doing

very well. Aleksy loved his school and his English was now better than his parents'. Thomasz the boy was talking more and almost sounding English. Franceska worked in a shop and she often brought gifts of fish. She said she was less and less homesick now.

Polly was better and enjoying being a mum. She had a growing stomach, which they told me meant there was another baby coming, another playmate for me! She, Matt and Henry were very happy. Henry was walking now and pulled my tail a lot, but in a fun, not mean way, so I tried not to mind too much. The biggest change was that they lived in a new house now, which happened to be right opposite Jonathan's. They were so much closer and the house they lived in wasn't as big as Jonathan's, but it was a lovely family home.

Claire and I both lived full time in 46 Edgar Road, with Jonathan. My idea to get them together had worked (although it took a while). It was the best plan ever, although they seemed to do it all by themselves, needing only a little help from me. They were so happy together, although Jonathan could still be grumpy and Claire would tease him. She wasn't scared of him and he treated her – and me – like royalty. Tasha visited all the time and they had other friends over, as well as Franceska's family and Polly and Matt. The house was busy and full, the way I had always thought it should be.

Claire and Jonathan called me their miracle cat because apparently I had done so much. I was growing quite an ego; the way they talked, you would think I had saved the world, not just helped four families. But apparently I had, and my life was all the better and richer for it.

As we settled into a routine which worked for us all, I had much to be thankful for: my friendships, my family, the love that surrounded me. My days of wandering the streets in fear, dodging cars and dogs and feral cats, scrabbling for food and shelter, were so far behind me that sometimes it felt as if that life had happened to another cat. But I knew it had happened to me, because my past was always with me. The tears and the fear, and the way my families had needed me, had become a part of me. I would never forget Joe and what he had done to me because, although it had cost me a lot, it had given me so much more. I would never forget when Aleksy came back from school with a certificate because he had written about his best friend, which was me. I would never forget Franceska saying that being in England had been so hard at first but that I had made it easier. I would never forget Claire saying I had saved her, and Polly saying the same. I would never forget that Jonathan teased me for turning him into a cat lover and telling Claire that I had saved him from the awful Philippa. I would never forget my long journey here, and I just hoped that the hard bit of it was now over and my relaxation could begin.

Because I was still happiest being a lap cat, and I now had the perfect number of laps to sit on. At night, I would sometimes go out and look at the stars. I would look at the sky and hope that Agnes and Margaret were up there somewhere, winking at me, because although I had apparently done a lot of good things since I lost them, I had only done it because of the love and lessons they had taught me. And I was a better cat for them and for everything I'd been through. And that, I had learnt, was how life worked.